Acknowledgement of Country

RMIT students, teachers and contributors acknowledge that this anthology was produced on the land of the Wurundjeri people of the Kulin nation. We pay our respects to Elders past and present. We recognise that sovereignty was never ceded. We acknowledge the rich tradition of storytelling of First Nations peoples in this nation.

Always was, always will be Aboriginal land.

What You Become: an anthology is published by Clover Press, an imprint of the Associate Degree in Professional Writing and Editing at RMIT University, 23–27 Cardigan St, Carlton 3053, Victoria, Australia.

ISBN: 978-0-6487056-4-2

ebook ISBN: 978-0-6487056-5-9

All rights reserved.

This publication and the individual creative works may not, in whole or in part, be copied, photocopied, reproduced, translated or reproduced in any electronic medium or machine-readable form without prior written consent of the publisher and the author(s).

Collection © Professional Writing and Editing at RMIT 2023.

Individual contributions © individual authors.

Page designer and typesetter: Shaun Jury

Cover designer: Darren Holt

Printer: IngramSpark

A catalogue record for this book is available from the National Library of Australia

ABOUT CLOVER PRESS

Clover Press publishes work from the RMIT Professional Writing and Editing programs. The clover, a humble, charming, resilient little plant, spreads far and nourishes many. Its distinctive three-lobed leaves perfectly capture the strength of these programs, integrating the three key areas of writing, editing and publishing.

This name is also inspired by Arthur Clover, a longstanding teacher who retired in 2015. Arthur had two influential mantras:

Always Put Students First; and Always, Always, Drink it While it's Fizzy!

The Clover Press logo was created by PWE graduate Ella Dyson.

What You Become:

an anthology

Contents

Introduction

Claire G. Coleman

Short stories sit firmly in the foundation of prose; they're the form we first learn when we tell a story, when we learn creative writing. We learn the basic form of short stories when we learn to spin a yarn as a child, learn how to tell a joke (because a joke is just a short story with a punchline). It's the form we're taught when learning to be writers, when we're developing our skills, and it's typically the first thing a new writer has published as they're learning their trade and working towards their first book.

In times past, literary journals were the best opportunity for new writers; write something powerful and short, then submit it and you *might* get first sight of your name in print.

Things have changed over the years; the literary journals that gave the authors of times past their first chance at publication have gone the way of the dinosaurs. It's now all online and microfiction, posts and socials. Short stories in a formal sense have faded into the background; for many writers their first ever published work is now a novel. But the short story should not be underestimated. Some of the best works of prose in history have been short. There's a power and a challenge in expressing a narrative in only a few words, which makes a short story powerful to the reader and insightful for the writer.

It often surprises even me that it can be harder to write a quality short, short story than something longer; that the shorter a word count limit the harder it is to reach perfection. Yet it's constraints and challenges that make our work more powerful.

Poetry can be even more challenging, and therefore more powerful; it's the power of words carved down to the purest of forms, words that stab straight into the heart without needing to touch the edges. Poetry is what many of us choose to learn first when wanting to be a writer, so it's frequently underestimated; in reality it is, perhaps, like scales for a musician or running for an athlete, the thing we must do to become better.

Poetry is not just slam poetry or Instagram poems; poetry is the language of the soul.

This collection of short stories and verse is proof of the skill and determination it takes to write shorter, more powerful works. The writers have wielded words like a scalpel, carving time into moments, the precise moment that's needed to tell the story and to break your heart, but no more.

To put it simply, and perhaps allow myself to be a bit trite, I'll use an old saying to describe the power of shorter stories and poetry: 'good things come in small packages' and then quote my parents who always used to follow that with 'and so do dynamite and poison'. That's what great short works are: good things in small packages that are sometimes dangerous (mostly to our equilibrium and in a good way) and might, if we're really lucky, explode.

CLAIRE G. COLEMAN (she/her) is a Noongar writer who's based in Naarm. She was born in Western Australia and her family have belonged to the south coast since long before history started being recorded. She writes non-fiction (*Lies Damned Lies*), essays, poetry and fiction (*Terra Nullius*, *The Old Lie* and most recently, *Enclave*). Follow her @clairegcoleman (Instagram).

Medical Certificate

Elle McFadzean

Who decided it was a good idea to make swimming classes compulsory? Especially for teenage girls.

We stood in a line outside the change room. Skinny legs, knobbly knees, cellulite, stretch marks, body hair, goosebumps, tampon strings, colourful caps and black one-pieces.

We all felt like monsters in our skin, but I was the only one who really was a monster.

I wrapped my arms around myself. I needed to get out of this. My parents thought swimming classes would be good for me – character building. They said they'd feel better knowing I wouldn't drown. That was a lie – they knew I could swim.

Drowning was the least of my worries.

I'd tried writing a note, forging their signature. *Yen is excused from swimming classes due to her period.* But Ms Turn told me to wear a tampon. Then I'd tried: *due to a medical condition.* But apparently I needed a medical certificate. Like I was ever going to get that. My condition wasn't something I could prove in a doctor's office, and without proof… who'd believe me?

Ms Turn blew her whistle. 'All right girls, listen up. We'll start with your choice of stroke. Two laps for your warm-up. Get going.'

Slowly, my classmates waddled to the edge and crouched down to feel the water. Karina squealed. 'It's so cold!'

'Once you're in, you'll get warm,' said Ms Turn. She clapped at them to hurry up.

I didn't move. I stood there watching as, one by one, the girls climbed down to sit on the edge. Then, still squealing at the temperature, they slid in, until I was the only one left.

'Yen, get over here,' said Ms Turn.

I trudged over. The concrete floor was cold and slimy, with puddles and strands of hair.

'In you get. You can use the ladder if you want.' She pointed to my left. Andy had twisted her legs through the pool ladder rungs and was floating on her back.

'Come on, Yen,' Andy yelled up at the ceiling.

Others joined in.

'You get used to the temperature,' Ursa yelled.

But the temperature wasn't my issue.

'I can't,' I said to Ms Turn.

'Course you can,' she said. 'I heard you used to swim every day.'

Who'd— Mum. But she didn't know that the first time I'd had a bath after getting my period, things had been different.

'Not anymore,' I said. 'Please. You can give me detention, but I can't—'

'Detention? No. You just need to get over—'

I felt hands shoving my shoulder blades. Panic set in and I pushed back, but it was too late. My toe stubbed the tiled edge, my arms flailed wildly and my chest toppled forwards.

I hit the pool with a loud splash.

Water gushed around me in swirling bubbles. I fled for the surface. There was still time. My limbs were weakening, turning to jelly, but *there was still time.*

I broke the surface with a gasp. Ms Turn was berating Andy. Everyone else was shouting, swimming towards me. I hardly saw them. I was too far gone to pull myself up onto the edge, but—

The ladder was close. I could make it.

I gripped the lane rope and hurled myself over it. Ursa was sitting on it and fell backwards, but I was already reaching for the next. I grabbed it, then lost my grip, fingers turning boneless.

I ducked underwater, but it was too late. I heard the softened echoes of my classmates yelling 'Yen!' in fright and worry.

And then in fear.

I propelled myself away from them, but there was nowhere to go. Tiled walls met me in all directions. Naked legs kicked in my periphery, trying to flee.

For every beat my heart pounded, faster and faster, my skin retreated, turning thicker and spongier. My legs multiplied and stretched to the pool floor, while my body compressed, squeezing my organs into themselves. As I broke the water's surface, I screamed, but it was a roar that tore from lines upon lines of pointed teeth.

High-pitched screams rang around me. I roared again.

I reached for the side of the pool but missed. A suctioned tentacle slithered across Karina's shoulder as she ran for the change room. She recoiled, tripped and fell back in, plunging underwater.

My limbs reeled, winding the water, desperately trying to grip something but instead forming a whirlpool beyond my control. Girls spun around me, lane ropes tangled in my tentacles and waves struck the walls. Ms Turn threw noodles and floaties in, but they were flung back out. A giant flamingo knocked her over. Tammy went flying into the lower diving board on a sprinkled doughnut.

The diving boards. The higher one extended over the pool within reach of where I was now held down, victim to the momentum. I stretched a tentacle up. It just reached. My suckers pressed to the underside, and it was enough for me to pull myself higher, for another tentacle to curl around the rail in a death grip.

I kept pulling, paying no attention to what was happening around me because *I had to stop this*. And I had to get out of the water to stop this.

With one last heave I hung from the diving board upside down, my limbs shaking as it violently bounced up and down and up and down. I slid higher, twisting around the board until I was perched above it. My limbs contracted, chest lengthened and fingers turned strong enough to grip the bouncing edge.

Girls were crying, still trying to escape the water. Ms Turn was blowing her whistle, tapping each girl on their shoulder as they fled past her into the change room. She went over and helped Tammy up, escorting the last of my classmates away. All the while, I watched through glassy eyes.

The floor was flooded, pool half empty. The ceiling looked like a chess board, foam panels floating below. Wall tiles were cracked and coated in mucus.

Eventually, Ms Turn came back. She looked up at me and cleared her throat. In a shaky voice, she said, 'You can go get changed now, Yen. And you can be excused from swimming classes.'

ELLE MCFADZEAN (she/her) writes young-adult and middle-grade fantasy novels. She has a background in architecture and a particular interest in worldbuilding. Her desk is covered in books, plants, cliché motivational quotes, literary magazines and sketched plans of imaginary cities. Visit ellemcfadzean.com to find out more.

How to Tell if It's Raining

Alexandra Mushta

Drizzle is my enemy. Without the *tip tap* on a tin roof to alert me, I can't quite tell if it's raining. Sure, a deluge doesn't go unnoticed, or even a moderate shower, but if it's spitting? Forget it. Short of stepping into the great outdoors and feeling the droplets on my skin, it's nigh on impossible. I rely on the pitter-patter, the hushed conversation happening on my roof. It clues me in, confirms my suspicions; my ears are finely tuned to the staccato melody of rain spitting on the earth before it decides to fully unleash itself. This is because when I look outside, it always looks like it's spitting.

I have visual snow. It's a recently discovered condition that envelops one's vision in a layer of static. I'm not sure if I've always had it, or if one day I suddenly noticed the infinite, pulsating dots, so overpowering that they had blocked out any earlier memories. There is no cure, no respite – just begrudging acceptance.

To me, the pulsating black and white doesn't resemble the peaceful flutter of a flurry. The world flickers like a broken TV; maybe my brain is broken in the same way. All being said, it's not *terrible;* there are degrees to the static, with mine being relatively easy to ignore.

The constant presence in my field of vision is more pronounced on swathes of single colour: a white wall, a clear blue sky, a shroud of solid black night. It's not so bad with patterns, or with busy graphics.

The snow throws a blanket over the other visual noise around me. If anything, the loudness of the modern world, the metropolises that never rest, pulls focus and provides a moment of respite – like snow calming after a blizzard.

But I yearn for the night sky; to gaze up above and be sure it is the stars that are truly twinkling, aglow with their cosmic power, and not an inconsistency in my brain. Night is the most difficult of the solar times. The curtain of darkness provides an endless opportunity to disturb my sight. To me it's these small things, the things that people take for granted, like breathing, blinking, being. I crave clarity. The security of knowing my eyes aren't deceiving me.

It is estimated that there are 300 billion stars in the Milky Way; they say the sky is full and our eyes can't see all that's out there.

The sky looks fuller to me.

ALEXANDRA MUSHTA (she/her) is a Geelong-based copywriter, editor and proofreader. She also, on occasion, writes non-fiction and, on rarer occasions, fiction. She enjoys cooking, crocheting and consuming long, epic works of speculative fiction. Visit alexandramushta.com to find out more.

Kitchen Garden

clarisse e stevens

1.
we dig through linoleum
leave these unwashed dishes behind
dig the soil from our kitchen grout
afternoon sun bakes me and my
spatula slips from my grip
and the word spatula stops me
because it sounds
like a flower

2.
in our   kitchen   garden
we will grow   spatulas
wake up and smell the   spatulas
she picked me a bouquet of spatulas
kissed   my   cheek
we   fell   asleep
beneath   spring   sky
& spatula   petals   fell
from   her   hair

3.

the spatulas are dying / summer heat browning / we press them in old books / compression to keep them / beautiful / compression for / remembrance

Illustrator: clarisse e stevens

CLARISSE E STEVENS (she/they) is a writer, poet and artist with a passion for speculative fiction. Many of her creations concern the natural world, queerness and existentialism. Find them @eyerites on social media.

Haircut

Lydia Schofield

This is an excerpt from a larger work.

It feels like a betrayal to bring Ravi with me instead of Zan or my mum. But he's the one who recommended the barber and somehow, it feels right for my newest friend to be with me for this new step. The barbershop is a few blocks up the hill from the cinema, so Ravi and I walk up after a shift. Its facade is painted a crisp white, with a rainbow barber's pole out the front. A sign painted across the front window reads, *All genders welcome – affirming haircuts inside!*

I pause on the footpath. It's right there, out in the open. It shouldn't, but that little fact stirs something in me. Half fear, a little excitement and a third, buzzing thing I can't quite name.

Through the window, there's a customer getting their shaggy pixie cut dyed bright green and another having their long hair and beard trimmed. One of the hairdressers wears bright pink pants and the other is more punk, with spiky earrings all the way down their ear and red streaks through their hair. I watch them for a moment before Ravi nudges me.

'We can walk around the block or stop for a coffee first, if you need.'

I shake my head and take a step forward, just as a tall person with short, shaggy hair and sunflowers on their overalls bursts out of the barbershop. The bell above the door tinkles as the person catapults into Ravi, hugging him tight.

'Hey, man,' they say, 'I thought I only just cut your hair.'

Ah, this must be Moss, the hairdresser Ravi told me about.

'You did.' Ravi waves at me dramatically. 'I've brought a friend with a mission.'

My cheeks burn. 'I don't have a mission.'

'That's alright, hun,' Moss says. 'You don't need a mission, just an idea. Some reference photos help too?'

'I've got those.'

'Amazing!' They wave their hands at me like they want to start fussing with my long hair immediately, before throwing open the door and holding it open for us. 'Let's make some magic,' Moss whispers as I step past them into the shop.

My chest feels lighter as I sit down. When Moss starts fiddling with my hair in that way hairdressers do – mussing it up and holding out the ends – they don't say, 'Oh, what lovely long hair you have,' like all other hairdressers I've had before. There is no, 'What a shame to cut all of this off.' Instead, they say, 'Your hair's pretty healthy, so well done on that. What would you like me to do with it?'

My hands shake as I pass them my phone with my reference photos from 80s movies and hipster queer girls. Through the mirror, I see Moss's face light up.

'Will this be your first mullet?' they ask, pure excitement in their face.

I nod and they squeal, handing me back my phone. 'Eddie, this is going to be so good. I promise you.'

Maybe it's just hair and maybe I'm overthinking the whole thing, but as Moss snips and sprays and works on my hair, something in me grows brighter and louder. I sit up taller. Ravi has taken the chair beside me, and he chats to Moss as they work. Every time he catches my eye, we both grin like Cheshire cats. I can't help it.

I read an article, during one of my late-night Google spirals, about the history of short hair as a lesbian symbol. As something that connects us with each other, all the way back through history to the Ancient Greeks. As I watch my brown hair fall onto the scuffed linoleum below, I can almost feel that thread of connection stretching out. I'm linked to all those women who came before me, the Victorian ladies in top hats and tails, the wartime land army girls, the slogan T-shirt-wearing feminists, the Dykes on Bikes at Midsumma. As Moss swishes the black cape off me and I see my new hair, my short, shaggy hipster mullet. I float above my seat, completely untouchable. Completely right.

><><

On the train ride home, I wonder whether the other passengers can sense my transformation. They don't know me, but can the man reading the paper feel the energy fizzing at my edges? Can the woman rocking the pram back and forth tell that I finally look like myself? My nerves only kick in as the train pulls into my stop and the reality hits me. I have to show my mum, who didn't even know I was going to get a haircut, that I've cut off nearly all my hair.

I drag my feet through the backstreets to my house and pause on the top step. Inside, I can hear my parents shouting at the telly, which must mean the footy's on. A deep breath. A key in the door. A few short steps to the lounge room. I stop in the doorway and wait for my mum to look over at me. It takes a second, but then her eyes meet mine and her jaw drops.

'Edna, what—'

'Hey!' Dad is up off the couch and standing in front of me before Mum can finish. He lets out one of those long, slow breaths that are terrifyingly unreadable before a grin blooms on his face.

'Kid, this is unreal,' he says, wrapping me into a tight hug.

When he lets me go, Mum is standing beside him. She rolls her eyes, smiling, 'You could've let me cut your hair.'

As she hugs me and then fusses with my hair, playing with the ends that flick away from my face, I realise I do know what that buzzing feeling was before. It's come back now, fizzing in my lungs and my heart and choking up the back of my throat: pride.

LYDIA SCHOFIELD (she/they) is a writer and artist from Melbourne. Their middle-grade and young-adult fiction explores themes of friendship and belonging (and sometimes features spaceships and magic). Lydia was shortlisted in Hachette Australia's Prize for Young Writers two years in a row and has been published in Catalyst and WhyNot. They can be found @scho.lydia (Instagram).

My Wife, the Vegetarian

Christiana Perdis

I've always hated vegetarians. They're too stringy, too cold, their blood too thick and clotted.

We used to joke about it, me and my wife. 'I love my dinner warm and gushing,' Margie would say with a twinkle in her eye, chin wet from burying her fangs into the aorta of our latest meal. She was so beautiful in those moments, dripping red onto the dirt of our forest floor, her translucent body glowing from the moonlight passing through it.

My wife is a vegetarian now.

Her ex-coffin-mate, Ilya, had put her up to it – that woman always was too fascinated with her food. She'd returned from her underseas trip almost two decades after our last meeting, her body opaque and wrinkled from walking along the ocean floor, her eyes a rich turquoise. The restrictions put into place post-9/11 had made air travel impossible for our kind, and we'd assumed prolonged exposure to the dark depths of the sea had affected her vision, and irises in turn. But as we began to lament underwater travel for its terrible toll on the corpse-body, Ilya was quick to correct us: 'My dears, I've gone vegetarian.'

I'd snorted, disbelieving. 'Fad diets are for humans, not us.'

Margie had agreed with me at the time, giving Ilya a wry smile that should've ended any further discussion.

It didn't.

Ilya told us of her travels, centring her tales around the vegetarian community she'd found in India – our kind, not human, though her new diet soon allowed her to live among even those creatures. She'd learned to sustain herself on the fluids found in trees. I'd remained unimpressed, disgusted even. I'd thought Margie would too.

She's been a vegetarian for three years now.

Ilya had told her it was best to quit cold turkey – or, in our case, no turkey. No humans, either. She'd stuck around only long enough to teach my wife how to drain a trunk of its sap and how to mix it with the thicker crimson resin found in the pine trees that populated our forest.

'Resin stops the human cravings,' Ilya had said on her last day with us. 'Pine may not taste as good as arjun tree, but it'll do the trick. What really matters is the sap – that's where you get all the good nutrients. Think of it like the blood of trees.'

I'd rolled my eyes.

Ilya had smirked, the tips of her fangs peeking through. 'Something to say?'

'The blood of trees? Are you kidding me? Trees don't bleed. Trees don't have arteries to bleed *from*.' I'd turned to Margie, a pleading note entering my voice. 'There's no *gushing*.'

The barest hint of doubt twisted my wife's features.

'They don't cry out as you sink your teeth into their neck. They don't even *have* a neck! And they—'

'Enough,' Ilya said, rolling her eyes. 'Margie, dear, don't let this brute sway you. And don't let me either. Remember, you can always go back to eating,' her nose wrinkled, 'human. If you really want to.'

Margie took a deep breath, pushing her shoulders back in a determined stance. I knew I'd lost before she even spoke. 'I just want to try it.' She gave me an uncertain smile, her eyes pleading with me to understand.

I forced a nod. 'Okay.'

Ilya rolled her eyes and pointed a sharpened nail at me. 'Make sure she drinks the sap.'

I barely restrained a snarl.

'You know, Margie would be better off if someone did this *with* her.' Ilya's thin lips drew into an unusually soft smile. 'I think you'd actually like being vegetarian if you—'

'Walk away,' I said, baring my teeth. 'Or I chase you out.'

Her laughter caught in the wind, taunting me long after she'd left.

><><><

Margie stayed home the next time I went to town – it was the first time I'd hunted alone in over two centuries.

The stars were dim that night, and there was a new moon darkening the sky. The first human I came across was stumbling, smelling of liquor and all too happy to lean on me. It should have been an easy kill. I guided him to my car, laughing along with his stupid mumbled jokes and restraining the urge to caress his beefy neck. Then his girlfriend found us. She gave a long-suffering sigh and wrapped his other arm around her, thanking me for my 'help' over her shoulder as she herded him towards their car. I should've followed them. Killed them both before they walked beneath the next streetlight – one for Margie, one for me. But Margie wasn't with me. And I'd forgotten how to hunt without her.

By the time I remembered, the couple was long gone.

The cicadas had grown quiet by the time I found a lean little morsel jogging on the outskirts of town. I took a few sips from their bare wrist – I get snacky after midnight – before stashing the bleeding human in the boot of my car. The intoxicatingly coppery scent taunted me the whole drive home.

I parked on the edge of our forest. Margie wasn't waiting for me. I found her near our grave, gnawing on a tree trunk, her fangs like spiles letting runny amber liquid trickle down her throat. Beneath the moonlight, her irises were bright turquoise like Ilya's. We continued to eat in silence; her hugging the tree, me hugging my human.

><><

I miss sharing breakfast with my wife. I miss kissing her, mouth wet and smearing red everywhere.

Her skin is opaque now, and hard like bark. As we lay together in our double-coffin, I miss seeing Margie's blackened organs pressed against mine, separated only by the thin membranes of our translucent skin. I miss talking the day away with her, buried too deep for the sunlight to touch us. Sleeping with her as sleep remained impossible for us both.

Now sleep only remains impossible for me.

CHRISTIANA PERDIS (she/her) is a writer based in Naarm. Her speculative fiction short story 'Nancy' has been published in *AntipodeanSF*, and she's currently working on her first fantasy novel. More about Christiana's writing can be found at christianaperdis.com, @christianaperdis (Instagram) and @XianaPerdis (Twitter/X).

Growing Pains

Upani Perera

For your whole life, your clothes have been too big. It started with hand-me-downs from your sister. Always the ugly stuff that she doesn't mind getting rid of – the cute clothes stay in the back of her closet until they get forgotten about. Then it was skirts from your mum and jumpers from your dad. They always fit you just a little bit off – too loose at the waist, the sleeves are too long, the neckline too stretched out. And you hated it, wearing other people's clothes, never being able to grow into your own.

><><

Do you remember your first day of high school? You felt like the smallest person in the world – your dress went down past your knees, your blazer three sizes too big and the building was a maze. You got lost on the way to your first Japanese class and the teacher hated you for the rest of the term. Your clothes were too big on purpose this time. 'Growing room' is what the lady at the uniform shop called it. 'Before you know it, that blazer will be fitting you like a glove,' she promised. It sounded like a joke at the time.

When did your clothes start fitting you? Except they don't really fit well, they just fit different. Too tight at the shoulders but too wide at the bust. Your jeans are still too big at the waist, but the hems don't reach your ankles. You wear them too big on purpose now because you don't want anyone seeing your body. Don't want anyone seeing *you*. If anyone looked closely enough, they would see the bones stretching, muscles stretching, skin stretching taut. Nerves burning and you don't want anyone to ever touch you; you want to live in your mum's arms forever. Your ribs spreading open to make room for the ever-expanding universe that lives in your heart.

As a kid, growing was a gift, a miracle. Your parents letting you stay home alone for the first time, riding a bike without training wheels, your first sip of wine at a family gathering. Every month, your mum would make you stand against the doorframe of the laundry; you'd stretch your back and crane your neck as high as you could while keeping your heels on the ground, trying to make yourself as tall as possible. You grow with each measurement – gaining three centimetres, two, one – until all of a sudden, your dad isn't the tallest man on Earth anymore. He's just a man.

><

You're a liar and a con artist – pretending you know the rules, but you're just copying everyone else. Don't be a slut, but you can't be too prudish; don't try too hard, but you can't not try at all; don't be too smart, but you can't be too dumb. None of it makes sense but somehow everyone seems to know these rules. Everyone except you. But you have always been an observer before anything else, and if there's one good thing about getting older, it's that it gets easier to see – everything is dull and less blinding, no longer in the technicolour of childhood. You watch people and you copy – monkey see, monkey do – and you play along, biding your time until you can finally figure it out. *If* you figure it out.

⋙⋘

You meet a girl who eats sunflower seeds. She offers one to you and you take it. It makes a flower bloom in your chest. She kisses you during a game of truth or dare and it's like nothing you've ever felt before. There are fireworks under your skin, and your heart's a bomb. You feel like you've done something terrible, like stolen from your grandma or pushed someone down the stairs. You could kiss her forever. It's your biggest shame. There's a boy who's lived next door to you for as long as you can remember. You used to make mud pies and race toy cars. One day he asks you out and when you turn him down, he goes around school calling you a slut, a dyke, an insecure virgin. You never fully trust boys again.

⋙⋘

You feel like someone's robbed you of something you can't quite name. The movies say growing up is *electrifying*. You're finding yourself, you're a child and an adult at the same time, you're a butterfly coming out of its cocoon. But you don't feel like any of that. You're just a girl. Where was your coming-of-age road trip? How come you never got to sneak out and go to parties? Your parents put you down one day and never picked you back up and you're the only person alive who doesn't know what they're doing and your sister doesn't love you as much as she used to and none of your clothes look good on you and the world is ending and no-one cares. Why doesn't anybody care?

But, here's the thing, you'll be okay. You won't know this for a long time, but you'll be *okay*. You'll learn to love your brain, your body, yourself. You'll learn the flowers blooming in your chest were love; you'll cough them up and give them to everyone who planted a seed in your lungs. You'll learn the secret that everyone learns when they grow up – that everyone else was making it up as well. No-one has it figured out and nothing is as dramatic as it seemed but that's what being a teenager is. It's thinking you're the smallest thing on Earth, but that you're also the centre of the universe; it's knowing nothing but thinking you know everything; it's caring too much about everything until the smallest thing feels like the world's ending. But someday you'll stop swimming against the ocean of time and start floating along with it, and maybe everything's not as bright as it once was, but it's still beautiful anyway. And you'll grow into your clothes, and you'll be okay.

UPANI PERERA (she/her) is a Sri Lankan-born writer based in Melbourne. She writes about real-life, lesbians and being eternally seventeen years old. Visit @up.cp (Instagram).

The Kiss

Isabelle Weiskopf

This is an excerpt from a larger work,
The Haunting of Gwendoline Jones.

Upon the plateau we follow our ritual. Lay our towels out on the rocks (mine yellow, hers pink), unceremoniously strip off our uniforms and lather each other in coconut suntan. This is our pilgrimage.

The straps of Margaux's teal bikini top have been visible beneath the crisp white collar of her school dress all day, sending the boys mad thinking about what lies beneath. There are some who would die to trade places with me, to share these moments with her. In instances like this, I know that I'm special. *Chosen.*

We jump, squealing and shrieking, into the river.

The water closes over my head and I'm submerged. This is my favourite part. For a second I'm weightless, a silver fish that has never known its own gravity. I blow a stream of bubbles up, sinking further down, watching my air break the water's shining surface. I'm still. Calm. Perfectly, incandescently content, and it's nice not to think about all the things I can't have. The people.

The person.

Then, I'm out of air.

Back above the water, Margaux is drifting lazily on her back, body held aloft by the gentle arms of the water.

The light catches her hair, making a gauzy halo from the long tendrils that stretch out beneath her in the soft waves. I love her like this, when she thinks no-one is watching. She looks so young, so light. No bitterness or hardness weighing her down.

I swim over to her, marvelling at the scene. If I could paint, I would capture this moment; Ophelia drowning peacefully in her watery grave. I swoop my arms under her neck, her legs, so that I'm cradling her. I see her eyes crack open, drowsy with sunlight.

'Hey there,' she says. A smile plays at the corners of her lips. 'Wanna take me away?'

I smile and swish her body around in the water. It feels safe here, with her. Her body is warm in mine, and I hold her tighter. 'I'll take you wherever you want to go,' I say, knowing that it's the truth.

'Do you mean that?' Margaux asks.

'You know I do.'

'Be careful with the promises you make me, Gwen,' she says.

'Or what?' I ask.

'Or,' she says, just as she splashes water in my face, 'I'll ruin you.'

I shriek and let her body go in revenge. She sinks into the water, curling away from me. 'You bitch!' I laugh. Intent on victory, I dive down after her and wrap myself around her body. She's squirming like a fish, trying to get to the surface, but I won't let her. We thrash around under the water, wrapped up in each other, struggling in slow motion.

I like the way her body is moving against mine, all hard thrusts and grappling movements. I hold her tighter. She won't win this one. Suddenly, I feel her body go still. She's not fighting anymore. Her arms loop around me, her hands coming to rest at the nape of my neck. She's drawing me closer, not pushing me away.

I open my eyes and she's there, right in front of me, staring through the gloom. She looks like a mermaid, ready to send me to an early grave with a watery kiss.

I bring her closer. Her skin slides over mine in the water, supple and slick. Her other hand roams around my waist, my hips, my thigh. I am wrapped around her and she's wrapped around me. I let myself touch her in all the places I can't above the water, all the places I've thought about touching her. We're woven together. Intertwined. Inseparable.

I can't breathe, not because my lungs are burning for air but because she's looking at me. She's looking at me and I don't care that I can't breathe, because our faces are so close and her eyes don't stray from mine. I'll stay here with her. Forever.

I reach out and let my fingers drift across her face, let my thumb graze softly over her lower lip. Her body shudders. Locked there, the moment stretches on for years. I can almost feel her heart pounding in her chest. Or is that mine?

Margaux untwines her arm from mine and I think she's going to kiss me but instead she delicately wraps her fingers around my throat. She squeezes softly. I jolt, blowing out air in surprise. Feel the moment end, the years rushing back to seconds. I unwrap my legs, my arms. Unwrap myself from her.

Her hand around my neck tenses. For a moment, I wonder if she's going to let me go. But then she does, and I'm racing towards the surface. Towards the air. Away from the liminal space where all is possible. Away from her.

My head breaks the surface and a second later so does Margaux's. We're breathing heavily, our bodies close, treading water. We don't say anything. We're staring at each other in an incredulous, almost wary way. I feel her hot breath on my face. It smells like the mango she ate at lunch and the thousand things we do not say.

'You okay?' she asks, like she doesn't know what just happened. Like we'd never existed in that watery world a million miles away from anyone. Like she hadn't felt my heart beating as fast as hers beneath her palm.

'Yeah,' I pant. I feel like I've run a race. 'You?'

Her smile cuts me to pieces.

'Oh, I'm fine, Gwen.' She turns and starts swimming to the water's edge. 'Just fine.'

ISABELLE WEISKOPF (she/her) is an actor and writer who completed her education at the Victorian College of the Arts Secondary School (VCASS) and Federation University on a scholarship. She debuted in the 2023 feature film *Remnant,* and is soon to film her second feature *Teenage Vertigo.* While studying, Isabelle is writing a horror novel; to read more visit weiskopfisabelle.wixsite.com/isabelle and @belle_weis (Instagram).

The Game

Kathryn James

Although there was a modest pile of gifts to unwrap, Ralph only cared about one. He just knew that the flat rectangle was exactly what he wanted.

Ralph really did know this, because he had snooped in his parents' wardrobe last week and seen the serene, smiling face of Jessica Fletcher (as played by Angela Lansbury) beneath the white plastic of a Coles New World bag. Mum would have picked it out specially.

But still, he tensed as he carefully unpeeled the sticky tape from the thin, reindeer-printed paper. The *Murder, She Wrote* board game was for him – wasn't it? He was the biggest fan in their family, could pick the murderer even before Jessica did. He was much better than his brother Morris, who pretended to prefer *Knight Rider,* but gave him Chinese burns in their shared bedroom whenever Ralph's prediction was right and Morris's was wrong.

And there was no unwanted surprise that Christmas morning. Ralph didn't care that he was banned from touching Morris's new remote-controlled car, or that his other presents were underwear and an ugly shirt. The game was his. He reverentially unpacked it, stroking the brightly coloured plastic rings and tracing his finger along the path between the rooms on the board.

Instead, the shock came on Boxing Day afternoon, when the family finally acceded to Ralph's pleading and sat down to play the game. Although he longed to be like the poised, perfect Jessica, bringing bad people to justice, Ralph discovered he was the murderer. No matter.

They all left the room, then returned one by one so the murderer could secretly pick their victim. Ralph selected his father's character, sliding a disc marked *DEAD* into the card.

Seated again around the table, Dad went first. Grabbing a handful of leftover nuts from a small glass bowl, he rolled the dice and immediately began to choke.

At first they thought the silent gesticulation was an act, but then Dad's face turned from red to blue and he thumped the table. Ralph and Morris sat frozen while Mum clutched Dad from behind, her thin arms encircling him below the ribcage. She finally screamed at them to call the ambulance.

It was almost midnight when they returned from the hospital, without their father. While Mum sat in the lounge sobbing, Ralph silently packed up the game pieces scattered across the table. As he covered them with the lid, Jessica's wide grin seemed to be judging him.

'You made it happen,' Morris hissed.

The cursed board game lay, abandoned, in the top of the wardrobe for the rest of his desolate childhood.

✕✕✕

After Mum finally died, Ralph suggested renting out the house for a while. But Morris insisted on selling, so he could get the cash he needed for his latest failing business.

It might be best, Ralph reflected, to split the proceeds and make a clean break. Morris was always going to be an arsehole; at least this way they wouldn't need to speak any more. And the money would be handy. Paul was due to retire soon. Perhaps they could finally take that trip to Paris.

'Why did you bring Rocco and Imogen?' asked Ralph.

'It's my weekend,' his brother grunted. 'The bitch wouldn't keep them.'

'Let's put them to work. There's still a lot to do.'

'Couldn't your *friend* come and help?'

'Paul has opera tickets today.'

After discarding endless piles of tattered towels from the wardrobe in their old bedroom, Ralph climbed the stepladder and began hauling down ancient Christmas decorations from the top shelf. His hands closed on a box. He pulled it out and blew dust off the lid. It was *the game*.

Jessica's red hair had faded to brown, and some kind of insect had attacked the blue cartoon mansion, exposing the cheap cardboard beneath.

'This one's for the bin, I'd say,' Ralph said, tossing it down. 'The op shop won't want it.'

'No, we can have a game with the kids later. Unless you're still scared of it?' Morris taunted.

'I didn't think children were into board games these days.'

'Kids are hardly your special subject, are they?'

'Whatever you say, Morry.'

When they stopped for lunch, Morris carried the game into the lounge and announced that everyone was playing. Rocco sullenly agreed only because his phone was out of battery. Imogen, engrossed in a book, was reluctant. She'd never even heard of *Murder, She Wrote,* but Ralph coaxed his niece into joining them.

'You get to kill people. Whoever you choose.' She looked up, wide-eyed, and he winked.

Ralph dealt the cards, furtively ensuring Imogen received the one denoting her as the murderer. Everyone else was a Jessica Fletcher.

'What do we do now?' asked Imogen.

'Everyone leaves the room, then the murderer secretly picks who they want to kill,' Ralph explained.

'Sounds gay,' muttered Rocco, and Morris cuffed him roughly.

When it was Imogen's turn, she giggled as she crept into the room. Outside the closed door, Ralph couldn't help but scrutinise his brother and nephew for signs of harm. But they were fine, of course. It was silly how the superstition had hung over him as a child. Finally playing the game felt like a release, a cleansing. A way to leave everything behind.

They crowded around the board. Ralph rolled the dice and moved his piece six places. Sweating a little, it took him a while to notice the pain radiating from his chest. As the pressure spread outwards into his arms, Ralph stood, then fell to his knees and dropped face first onto the flowered carpet.

Behind him, Ralph heard Morris swear. But he was already fading into unconsciousness.

KATHRYN JAMES (she/her) writes about parenting, society, places and little moments that change us. She's developing children's and adult fiction manuscripts. Kathryn works as a freelance copywriter and international development consultant. Her work has appeared in *Overland* online and *n-SCRIBE*. Find her at kathrynjameswriter. wixsite.com/home or @thejamsnarky (Twitter/X).

Wait and See

Madii Oakley

This is an excerpt from a larger work.

'So,' the doctor says, reading the back of the box, 'we're inserting your IUD today?'

The fact that he poses this as a question rather than a statement does nothing for my nerves. He reads the little paper instructions inside the box, checking to make sure all the bits are in there.

'Now you're aware of all the risks? It's very rare of course, but perforation, expulsion and ectopic pregnancies may occur after the insertion. Do you have any questions?'

'No. I've definitely done my research.'

'Okay great. So, there may be some irregular bleeding within the first three to six months. But this usually subsides. Some women stop getting their periods altogether. When are you due for your period?'

'Yep. Umm, I just had it about a week ago.'

'Hmm okay. Not ideal timing. Usually during ovulation is best because it's easier to get through the cervix. But, we can see how we go and, if we need to, we can reschedule.'

Reschedule? Absolutely not.

'I'll just quickly have a look at it.'

For a minute I think he's referring to my vagina, but to my relief he instead pulls out the device, studying it carefully.

'This will be my first insertion.'

Umm, what? Why would he tell me that?

I blink at him. 'Okay.'

'Don't worry, I've definitely done my research.' He winks as he repeats my words back to me.

I cringe and all I can muster is, 'Hm.'

'Alright. Let's go into the insertion room shall we?'

While I slip out of my clothes, I think about how trivial the gown is. They're just going to be looking under it anyway. Sitting up on the examination table with bent knees, I look from one leg stirrup to the other. I press my legs together firmly, keeping them where they are.

The doctor returns, this time, with his buddy, Nurse Matt.

They use medical jargon to explain to me what's going to happen, and I can feel my eyes glazing over.

'Once that's all done, we need to measure the depth of your cervix.'

There are different depths?

'That's where *this* comes in.' He holds up a long plastic device in his left hand. 'We'll measure how deep your cervix is so that we insert your IUD just the right amount. Okay?'

I want to scream.

'Mmmhmm.'

'Lying back for me, shuffling down a little bit… that's it. If you can place the soles of your feet together and let your knees fall out… great. Now I'm just going to lift the gown, okay?'

'Yep.' I can hear the frustration building in my voice, but I don't think he notices.

'Alright, just placing the speculum in.'

It's cold and chunky.

'Opening the vagina.' He looks over at Nurse Matt who's standing to my left, observing.

'Matt, can you hold this for me?'

At that moment I think I might hate them. Both of them.

Nurse Matt takes over prying me open and the doctor moves to the other side of the room, rummaging around. He comes back a few seconds later.

'Just a little cold here.'

The coldness is deep inside my lower stomach and I try hard not to contract. He's cleaning my cervix. *Is my cervix normal? What if it's too long? Too shallow?* Yet another thing I can be self-conscious about. *Yay.*

'Quick little pinch while we measure.'

He's struggling to get it in. Reaching up to where Nurse Matt's holding, he roughly repositions the giant metal tongs inside me. I grimace.

He tries again. 'There we are.'

The doctor removes the measuring tool and shuffles back to his station. I slump my head back into the chair and wait.

Nurse Matt is still holding my vagina wide open.

I wonder if a bug might fly up inside me and be trapped forever.

He's taking his time.

I look up. The doctor's back is to me. I lower my head again, being sure not to make eye contact with Nurse Matt.

'So, do you have all your Christmas presents sorted?'

You've got to be kidding me.

'Umm, I guess so. Have you?'

'No not yet. I've left it to the last minute again and now all the shops are super busy and it won't arrive in time if I order it online. So I don't know what I'm going to do.'

Aw, poor Nurse Matt.

I press my lips together and nod, wishing the conversation would end.

'I'm sure he won't be too much longer.'

Couldn't they have done this *before* opening me up? It definitely feels like they could've done it before.

'Sorry about that.' The doctor walks over, distracted by the IUD in his hands.

'Alrighty, let's get to the main event. Now, just a little sting.'

Holy. Fuck. I breathe deeply and slowly. It's somewhere deeper than I've felt before – achy *and* sharp at the same time. *Ow!*

'Bit of a pinch.'

Oh it's not done? *Shit, shit, shit.* I focus on controlling my breath, which seems to be the only thing I can control right now. The doctor does one last jolt without warning this time, and I try to stay as still as possible.

'All done.' He puts the insertion device on the little metal trolley next to Nurse Matt. The speculum's still inside me. *Get it out.*

'Now we'll keep you here for the next half an hour to make sure you don't have any immediate side effects, okay?'

I nod.

The doctor removes the speculum. *Finally.*

As they leave the room, I lie there feeling different from when I walked in. I convince myself this was the smart, responsible thing to do. Not *really* sure of the long-term ramifications, not *really* sure if I'm going to be a statistic or not. I gently rub my tummy. *Welp, you're in there now. Guess we'll have to wait and see.*

MADII OAKLEY (she/her) is making moves on Wurundjeri and Bunurong Country. A writer currently working on her debut novel touching on themes of identity, connection and the female experience. She's previously co-created an anthology of short stories and a nature zine. Keep your eyes peeled.

Stagnant

Chance Yun

The taste of the familiar starts fresh upon the tongue.

Cosy wooden houses with thatched roofs, beige and weathered from the elements. Small fields growing local produce, fenced in with low clay bricks. The soughing of wind through dense foliage is a lullaby, the arched branches of the trees are safety. She is only one among dozens who live here, generations content with repetition. Nobody has ever needed for anything.

The stream that runs through the village is a steady presence, nurturing them through childhood as much as a mother's milk. The girl dips her hands into the water, pulling up a clear mouthful to her lips; lets it wet her throat, slide down to sit coolly within her stomach.

She drinks, and tastes what she always has – comfort she has always known.

><><

The years grow hotter, the heat strong enough to make skin tender to the touch. The trees lose their limberness. Lush grass becomes faded and brittle, its fresh, earthy redolence absent from the air. These are not the only changes: most of those around the girl's age are gone now, having moved away without looking back.

Come with me, she was once urged, the amber of her friend's eyes shining golden in the light. Their hands had been entwined, a grounding connection. *Let's go out there together.*

But what is 'there'? she had wanted to ask, words caught behind her teeth. If she went, who would help tend to their shrinking fields, to the remainder of their elderly? Who would help prepare for winters, and toil in summers? What could she possibly contribute *out there* compared to what was *here* now?

She stays.

At dusk, the girl stumbles before falling to her knees at the stream's edge, dress pressed into the dirt. Her reflection ripples on the water's surface, bisected by a jagged stone, features warping. She stares back at herself before plunging her hands in to break the image.

She drinks, and ignores how the water no longer quenches her thirst.

><><

An urgency exists within her head, like a blaring siren muted by her skull. Tree bark sloughs off in rough, flaky sections. It litters the ground with decay. The harvest is poor, and now the remaining villagers consider their options. There's talk of culling pets to free up mouths to feed. There's talk of weathering it out. For her, there's talk of leaving.

You're still young, they say, familiar faces crinkled with familiar concern. *There's more for you than what's here.*

The water of the stream is shallow now, trickling over sage-green boulders, tepid against her skin. A stale sourness tinges the air. She trembles as she brings the heels of her palms to cracked lips, eyes locked onto the trees of her childhood. For the first time, the arched branches appear like gnarled claws, a cage above her head that obstructs the light.

She drinks, and forces herself not to gag.

×××

Where is 'there'? she wants to ask her friend.

The girl is curled up in her bed, both mind and body foetal. Her insides cramp and rebel, roiling with waves of pain. Outside, the fields are empty, soil eroded. The dryness and wind cut through what's left of the village, stripping the trees of their life. All that was once familiar and comfortable is rendered inaccessible.

The girl weakly licks her lips, the drag of her tongue catching against grooves that sting. Her heart thuds within a thin chest.

She shakes, and wonders about what exists outside of *here*.

×××

The stream is thin, now merely a discoloured dribble stubbornly creeping along its path. The taint of the water clings to the papery skin of the girl's hands. There's barely a handful, gritty and foul like a warning. It holds in the cup of her palms like a long inhale, still and foreboding.

And she lets it fall, sluicing between parted fingers, trailing down trembling wrists and bony elbows – grey-green tears from a dying land. It drips into the earth, onto the bare stones. It falls like tiny links of a chain.

She turns, and walks in search of something new – clear, sweet and fresh.

CHANCE YUN (she/her) is a tentative writer and editor based in Melbourne. Introvert, tea-loving and somewhat concerned about the state of her house because of her cats, she writes in an effort to make sense of her own convoluted thought processes. Email awriterschance@gmail.com to get in touch.

Cowboy George
and the Visitor

Erin Rose

Cowboy George relaxed into his patio chair and placed his cup of tea on the table beside him. A soft breeze blew across the cornfield, sending a rustle through the stalks. He stretched out his legs and settled in to watch the beautiful pinks and oranges of the sunset dance between the storm clouds gathering on the horizon. Moments like these made the hard hustle of farm life worth it.

As he turned to reach for his cooling tea, some movement within the growing shadow of the generator shed caught his attention. *Strange… there ain't no deer in these areas.* He shifted to get a better view without startling the critter, which was sniffing around some empty grain sacks by the shed door.

Cowboy George sat back and sipped his tea. It moved on all fours and definitely had fur, but… *no, couldn't be that a horse escaped.* With no interruption, the creature's sniffing got bolder, and soon Cowboy George heard the metallic pull of the door bolt.

No sir, that's enough brownnosing for tonight. If those electrical wires got chewed, he'd be in all sorts of trouble. Cowboy George stood and walked down the porch stairs, the jingle of his spurs making his presence known.

The furry form, startled, stood up on its hind legs like a man. It must have been over six feet tall and covered in dark green fur that looked a matted mess. The creature's eyes locked with his – *three* eyes, all glowing like tiny violet fireflies. In forty years of farming and herding the West Ranges, he ain't never seen anything like *that*! It made a noise that sounded like a pig crossed with television static and dropped back to all fours before running into the cornfield.

Cowboy George stood there, mouth agape. He was a man of many talents and knew a lot of things, even without any fancy book-learning. But this – this was something new. *Ol' Pappy always said when it comes to beasts, you need to choose the battleground, not them.* With no gun and the sun quickly fading, Cowboy George thought it best to collect his teacup and quietly retreat inside, locking the door behind him.

$\times\times\times$

The first thing Cowboy George did the next morning was go back to where he saw the creature. There were a series of tracks in the soft dirt around the shed, each imprint consisting of a half-moon-shaped pad surrounded by three triangular points. He followed the tracks down the road, where it seemed to have stopped by the horse trough for a drink.

The horses were huddled together at the opposite side of the pen, and the trough was unusually empty. A slimy purple film had grown across the water... Something told him not to touch it. *Water doesn't just go and change like that; this was the creature's doing.*

Now, Cowboy George wasn't a man of violence. He respected God's creations and even left the fox dens alone if they didn't kill his chickens. But he couldn't have his horses being spooked and their water being tainted. No, his violet-eyed guest needed to leave.

That evening, Cowboy George set himself up on the patio with his tea and a gun, and waited, eyes fixed on the shadows growing behind the shed. It wasn't long before the creature's bulking silhouette emerged, its three violet eyes glowing and bobbing softly with hesitant steps. The eyes moved from him to the shed door and back again. The hum of the generator seemed to grow as the creature approached.

Cowboy George stood. The creature stopped.

This time, however, it didn't run.

The two exchanged glances across the dusty expanse between them. Cowboy George's hand twitched, ready to draw his gun at the first sign of aggression. The creature looked towards the door and let out a mournful whine while pawing at the dirt.

Well, shoot. He hadn't expected this. Whatever this thing was, it seemed to be asking for help. But what in tarnation did it want from inside the shed? If he opened the door, was it going to charge in and make a mess? With what it did to the horse's water, he didn't want it sticking around.

He went to pick up the gun, but hesitated. He didn't have the heart. He'd always been a sucker for an animal with puppy-eyes.

Taking his tea instead, he made his way down towards the shed. The creature took a few steps back but didn't retreat further. It let out another static whine as it kept its eyes on Cowboy George, who cautiously opened the door and stood aside.

The creature's eyes glowed brighter as it trotted up, sticking its head inside the shed. It smelt something awful, like rotten eggs, and had sticks and leaves caught in its shaggy green and purple matted fur. Cowboy George recoiled in surprise as it opened its mouth and roared at the generator. The generator whirred louder, as if shouting back.

As the racket grew, the wind picked up and an orange light appeared above them in the night sky. Cowboy George covered his tea with his hand as a wall of dust blew towards him. By golly, that right there be a spaceship if he ever saw one! All shine and steel in the moment, but fast collecting a coat of farm dust.

A ramp extended down, and the creature wasted no time bounding over to it on all fours. It took one last look at Cowboy George before disappearing into the craft. The ramp withdrew, and in a flash, the ship shot up into the sky, gone before the dust had a chance to settle.

As Cowboy George watched in disbelief, he didn't notice the bloom of purple spreading across the ground where the ship had landed. Nor did he realise that the soles of his boots had picked up a coat of the slime as he headed back inside. After a few hours pondering the experience and whether he should report the event to the police, he retired to bed, tired and shaken.

><><

The next morning, Cowboy George didn't wake up.

It took another two days before someone noticed he was missing. By then, the potent ooze had engulfed half of the house and expanded into the cornfields, leaving a trail of rot in its wake.

The nightly news reported similar accounts across the country. As the contamination spread, so did chaos.

A *change* had begun, and it was relentless.

ERIN ROSE (she/her) is a space nerd who's always loved escaping reality through reading. Based in Melbourne, Erin is currently studying two degrees in science and writing, hoping to combine them in the future to share her passion for STEM with others.

The Oven

Brendan Mason

I walk down Oven Court holding my electric lamp aloft, letting the yellow beam illuminate the cobblestones, the twisted stone gutters and the wrought ironwork of dead gas street lamps.

Nobody lives in Oven Court. Most of it is the burned orange brick-back end of terrace housing. No windows. Two empty gibbets hang on either corner where it meets Belker Street. They are historical relics. In times past they were valued tools in the old justice system, now they are just symbols.

At the end of Oven Court looms a giant door with no nameplate. The Oven Building. As I approach, locks start to clatter and grind open, courtesy of the waiting doormen. The hinges groan as they push the heavy door and as I walk toward the deskman, he slides the guest book across his desk. He cannot see me; nobody lowly who serves in the Oven Building has eyes anymore. I scratch my name in the book and push it back to him. He takes it, says nothing. His lips are sewn shut.

I make my way through the corridors with some familiarity. Although my soul has never been here before, the body I am wearing has, and bodies always remember more than you think. Some of my duties require different bodies to maintain anonymity, which is important tonight. In my faith, God blames bodies for sins, not the souls who ride them. Tonight's meaty clothing is damned a hundred times over while my birthly flesh sleeps at home, blameless. One day I will ride it to the heavens.

Yesterday, I watched a man hang in the courtyard of the old Bonegate Prison. He was hanged the old way, stripped naked and hauled up off the ground until only his toes touched the dirt. While the strength in his legs held out, he lived, choking, but alive. I watched his face as the strength left his body, as he wriggled, and his face turned ever darker purple. He wrenched his hands free of their bonds and tore his fingernails on the rope. He couldn't help trying to live even though he had come to hate being alive. The body, you see. His mind rebelled against further misery, but his hands wanted to live. After he died, I made a passable sketch of his bloated face. My mother adored it and put it up in the parlour.

Now the hanged man's body is in one of our ovens. I peek through the glass and see him wrapped in a shroud, his hands across his chest. Heat shimmers across his body but the material of the shroud is heat resistant. I have timed my visit perfectly. He is nearly done.

The cooks open the oven. Ignoring the blast of heat, they haul out the tray with their thick cook's mitts, lay him on the slab and leave the room while I wait for him to cool. I sit in the corner and read a novel that a friend, and colleague, had gotten banned for obscene content.

I think we had the author shot... but I'd have to look it up.

After a while, the body starts to twitch and writhe. The hands claw at the shroud, tearing it away from his face. The diaphragm yanks at his lungs and hauls in bucketfuls of greasy kitchen air. Heels hammer against the tray and I hear his heart stammer into life, the ripple of blood in his veins.

He is alive. Again.

He chokes, hacks up fluid, rolls onto his side, coughs, and vomits. His breathing settles and he starts to cry. I realise suddenly and with displeasure that I had forgotten to bring a bookmark. I hope I remember the page I was on; I close the book and set it aside.

'Good morning,' I say. 'Welcome to a brand-new day.'

I always say that to him, no matter the time. He stops crying and sits up on the slab, holding the shroud so I don't see his genitals. I marvel at the durability of habits. He glares at me. I would describe him, but his appearance, like his name, is irrelevant. He looks worn out. Normally a freshly-baked person's flesh is filled with exuberance, something I can personally attest to, but he looks like the page of a book that has been crumpled and flattened out many times.

He swears at me, using words that were once obscene and extremely offensive but now are common language that even my mother might use without much care. Even priests use these words, but he still remembers them as venomous and so seeks to poison me. One day I will tell him he sounds like an old-fashioned ninny. But not today. It is still funny to me.

'Would you like something to eat?' I ask him. He swears again.

All we ever feed him is a dish that was once his favourite. We have it prepared with such care. It is all he eats now. It is all he has eaten for countless thousands of meals and while it remains as delicious and daring as it ever was, his tongue hates it, his throat gags at it and his stomach is queasy at the thought of it.

I ring a bell and the cooks come in to take him away, dress him, feed him and return him to his cell. More than four hundred years ago he did something to displease us. I do not know what and I do not care enough to find out.

All I know is this. He has been condemned to eternal life in prison. Once a year he is hanged, and life baked back into his body. Once a year he appeals his sentence and once a year we reject the appeal. His miserable life remains the same, forever and forever.

I hurry home, eager to continue reading my book.

BRENDAN MASON (he/him) is a freelance writer who specialises in horror. His long-term writing project is the Dieselpunk horror series, also known as Project Drowned Rat. He watches too much wrestling and not enough horror, but his mum still likes him.

Chaos in the Chrysalis

Emma Goodall

*L*oop, around, through and pull.
It sounds simple, right?

Not for the left-handed children of right-handed parents.

Learning to tie my laces was confusing business for my mother and me. I would study her hands, watch her *loop* with the left, *around* and *through* with the right. I memorised the actions – *loop, around, through and pull* – until I knew precisely how to tie the laces.

But when I mimicked her, the laces turned to weighted ropes in my tiny hands. My movements clumsy and unnatural, fingers working in frustration as they tried to do what they were told. *Loop* – left. *Around* and *through* – right. The result – a sub-par tie.

Perhaps it's why my favourite shoes were velcro runners, white with butterfly prints. No laces, no brain power or right-handed manoeuvres – just the soft crackle of hook meeting loop, and they were fastened.

It's interesting what things we remember from childhood, when a thought was a thought, an action an action, and the subtle disconnects between the two didn't mean all that much. It's only when you get older, when the disconnects are bigger, more frequent, that you start to understand the real meaning behind a moment.

Now, in my 20s, I still wear white runners. But they have laces, lack butterflies and give absolutely nothing in the way of arch support. They're the far less cool footwear of the corporate-casual scene I belong to now, which in truth is not a scene I ever thought I'd find myself walking through. You see, I may have learned to tie my laces, but I never quite tied the threads of thought and action into a neat little bow. I made a knot instead and frayed the ends – each a different solution to the same scenario, a multitude of answers to the one question and a series of possibilities that will likely never come to pass.

So when I'm living the life that lets me sit in a spring-sprinkled park on a Tuesday, cherry blossom backdrop, white runners on, and the only thing I feel is a weathered noose of thoughts, I wonder – why the hell am I here?

I'd been sitting on the grassy knoll for almost an hour, double the time it had taken me to find the 'perfect' spot. The first offered little protection from the sun, the second sprayed me with wind-blown pond water and the third *was* perfect, until I noticed the ant nest near my ankles. After three scouting attempts, I felt the imaginary stares of other park visitors as I hopped from one grassy patch to the next and heard their whispers as they mocked my dance of indecision. So I walked towards the little mound I'd eyed from the moment I stepped into the park, and I sat. The final spot. No more moving.

My intention was to read, to force myself into a fictional world that would seal off the tangle of frayed threads controlling my actions – the tangle that had formed the moment I stepped off the plane that got me here. There was the thread that wanted to drink sake in a cosy, low-lit bar, while another couldn't stomach opening the door; the one that just wanted to explore slowly in quiet solitude, while another needed to race until sleep would come easily; and the one that wanted to write on clean lined pages, while another stilled the hand that held the pen.

Then there were the others, the constants. They were the ones that needed boxing. Stories of bow-and-arrow-wielding heroes with a penchant for toxic faeries had recently been doing the trick. But as much as I tried, I couldn't get past more than a few sentences before my eyes wandered off the page, chasing the frays of that pesky tangle.

The routine wasn't new to me, but it shouldn't have been happening here. This place, this experience, this *step* toward the future, *this* was supposed to be what it was all for – the sleepless nights, weary muscles and nail-dented palms. It was to make my heart happy. Being here made my heart happy right? *Right?*

It did.

And once that was enough.

Now it's not.

I close the book and stuff it inside my backpack. Time to move on, to walk it off. Hold it together. I sit up straight, palms flat against the earth, and brace to push up. But my eyes lock onto the glassy surface of the little pond and I suck in breath until my nostrils burn and my chest hurts. This isn't part of the plan.

Push up. Come on.

Nothing.

Where will you go?

Exhale.

Move your legs.

Nothing.

It'll be over soon. Stay.

Inhale.

It won't be if you stay here. Move.

Exhale.

I look down at my white runners and move a finger to trace the seams.

Is this how it's supposed to be? Is metamorphosis just a pretty term for pain?

I follow the stitched path like an old cobblestone road until my finger finds a loosened lace bow. There it is. The moment.

There's only so long you can hold yourself together when chaos is the undercurrent to every thought.

I picture it – a rip, hear it – a tear. Velcro runners, white with butterfly prints.

I wonder if butterflies feel free when they emerge from the chrysalis. Or are they all too aware of just how short the rest of their life is?

EMMA GOODALL (she/her) is an all-things-words enthusiast, a writer and an editor. When she isn't off adventuring, Em is playing with stories in the travel space or pursuing her interests in memoir and fiction. If you ever find her little nook of thoughts on the internet, best not to tell her.

Mister Misery

Nietta

Old foe, you keep me company,
your thoughts and mine are one.
Sadden me, (wallowing!) it pains me,
to my head you hold a gun.

Mister Misery, you and I,
married to my mind.
Am I yours or
are you mine?

The flame I was,
you rain and storm.
A soul ignited, now,
cinders extinguishing.

No control, subdue me
with your weighted hug.
I drink from your cold,
as you drain my hot.

(In the furnace, melt away now.)
(Incinerate you. Incinerate you.)

Thou shalt pretend,
thy stage awaits,
my sadness is now,
my friend.

Old foe, please go, I can not
let go, heart's inferno raging on.
Take my flame like it is thine,

(Masqueraded all this time.)
(I am fine. I am fine.)

Mister Misery, you and I,
married to my mind.
Old foe, dear friend,
must we embrace?

Illustrator: Nietta

NIETTA (she/her) is a writer, poet and illustrator. She enjoys dipping her toes into genres such as horror, contemporary fiction and children's literature. On the side, Nietta loves to geek out and flex her creative muscles by creating video essays and analysis content. Follow her @NPCMedia (YouTube) and @niettea (Instagram).

Under Her Skin

Em Collings

The Selkie is the most stunning woman you have ever seen. She is as dangerous as the sea she walks from, with an anger that rivals that of the waves that crash against rocks, smoothing them over or shattering them. You knew that, but no matter what she did you always found yourself back by her side, even when she had run out of new ways not to deserve your trust.

She sits on your bed and asks you to braid her long hair. You trip over yourself to do it. You would do anything if the request came from her lips.

You don't dare use anything other than your stubby fingers to untangle her hair. There is intimacy in forgoing a hairbrush. She is wearing nothing but your old sweatshirt – her grey, spotted pelt coat hanging by a hook next to your door, always in her line of sight.

She knows you won't take it. You revere and fear her too much to ever make her angry. The coat is a reminder that she belongs to the ocean.

You are careful with the braid. If you tug too hard, there is a chance she will eat you alive or drag you into the icy ocean like the sailors who have hunted her. She has made sure humanity knows she is not to be trifled with. The last man to try to take her coat still haunts the bay he died in.

You have been luckier than others.

'Are you alright?' She shifts, and her hair slips from your hands so she can face you – her voice is like a song, something haunting. 'You're shaking.'

'I'm sorry.' You shouldn't look at her eyes. If you do, you won't be able to pull yourself back out. Her eyes are the most inhuman thing about her when she is in this form. They're a deep brown, taking up most of her sclera; the white peeks through only when she looks too far to the side. You can almost see yourself reflected in them.

'Why are you sorry?' She leans forward and cups your face, pressing her nose and forehead against yours. You shiver. She goes back to the ocean tomorrow. You're a terrible person... but you don't want her to go.

><><

You first met the Selkie when you were at your lowest.

You were with a friend. He had been kind, always kind. Until he wasn't. The ravenous hunger he kept to himself burst out like blood from a punctured artery, covering you in the horror of his greed. He took. He wasn't human anymore. A monster, driven by want.

The Selkie saw your pain, and she took pity on your fractured heart. There was an ache that ran deep into your bones and an exhaustion that consumed you. She didn't say a word, just wrapped her grey coat around you. With that you were safe. You would do anything for her if it meant feeling like that for even another moment.

She is the ocean – equal measures beautiful and terrifying with a rage that chips away at cliff sides and a calm that washes clean.

⋙⋘

'What's wrong?' she repeats, and you can't escape her gaze. She holds you close to her.

You sigh deeply. 'I don't want you to go,' you whisper. It feels as though you'll explode into a million pieces if you say it even a little bit louder.

'Then come with me,' she says.

Your eyes widen. You would never have expected her to invite you back to the sea.

At your silence, she curls into herself, pulling away from you, no longer feeling each other quite as much. 'It's just an offer, you don't have to come.'

'No, I want to, please, I promise I want to,' you stumble over yourself to try to reassure her, 'it's just that I'm not like you, I'm not made for this.'

She smiles, it's not predatory in the way you've seen her smile at others, it's much softer than that, reserved only for you in moments like this.

'That doesn't matter.'

The next morning, you both shuffle out of your house before dawn. You wrap yourself in the thickest woollen jumpers and coats you have, and she walks out into the snow with nothing but her coat around her shoulders.

When you reach the shore, she holds your hand and walks you into the water beside her. The brine laps at both of your ankles, and she presses a soft kiss to your cheek before taking both of your hands and leading you deeper and deeper. First your boots fill up, then your clothes soak through and finally your lungs swell. The sea foam swallows you both, but she isn't herself anymore, instead her familiar round eyes on the unfamiliar hulking mass of a seal. She doesn't let you float off; she is waiting for you to shift into something else too, something new.

You don't care about what you become. As far as you are concerned, you're just a pebble caught in her drift.

EM COLLINGS (they/she) is a creator with a special interest in horror, fantasy, sci-fi and gothic fiction. She's passionate about accessibility and ethics within creative and bureaucratic fields. They consume all manner of content from books and film to podcasts and video games.

The Great Switch

Aoife Niland

I was five years old when I learned about the Great Switch. Mr Sanchez-Li was looking to fill time before the end-of-day bell, and one of my classmates asked about it. When the bell dinged over the speakers, I rushed out of the classroom, bouncing with excess energy to tell Mum.

She stood by the back entrance of the schoolyard, near the sports shed that smelt weird. She leaned against the bright green fence line, fiddling with her fancy clicky-click black pen. I ran towards the gate, my bag hitting the back of my knees. The books inside thudded against my lunch box.

'Mum, Mum, *Mum*! I have something to tell you! I have something to tell you!'

She spun around with wide green eyes and a massive grin. I danced on the spot by the gate, the energy sweeping through me like a huge wave. Mum laughed, big and bright, as she stepped towards the gate and released me from the colourful jail for children.

I wrapped my arms around her, nuzzling into her soft tummy. I squeezed, and she yelped with a giggle.

'Hello to you too!' she exclaimed.

Mum took my bag off my shoulders and hooked it onto hers. She nudged me towards the car and opened the heavy sky-blue door.

'So, you had something to share with me, poppet?'

'Yeah, yeah, yeah! Mr Sanchez-Li told us about the Great Switch!'

I jumped into the back seat of the car, shimmying into the plush booster seat. Mum reached inside the car and fought with the seatbelt buckle for a few seconds before it clicked into place.

She asked, 'What did he tell you about the switcheroo?'

'Mum! It wasn't like any other switcheroo – it was the *Great Switch*!'

Mum chuckled under her breath, warming the top of my head.

'My apologies. What did Mr Sanchez-Li tell you about the *Great Switch*?'

'He said Australia used to be a big cake with red sand!' I said, chest puffed up like a cat who caught a canary.

'Australia used to be a cake?' Mum blinked several times before an amused *huff* left her lips. 'Do you mean Australia used to be a desert?'

'Yeah, a cake.'

'A cake is a *dessert*, sweetie. A desert is like a beach with no water,' Mum said. She kissed the top of my head before closing the car door, hopping behind the steering wheel. She started the engine and drove out of her spot. After a minute of silence, she asked, 'Did Mr Sanchez-Li say anything else about the Great Switch?'

'Umm,' I started, not wanting to be wrong again, 'he said that because of the Great Switch, the middle bit of Australia is just lots and lots of snow.'

Mum nodded. 'He's right. In fact, when I first moved here, Australia had the best beaches because it hardly ever rained in the summer!'

I looked out the window. The sky has always been a dreary grey, thick with clouds and constant drizzle. The first time I ever saw a parting in the clouds, the pure blue, I had thought it was the end of the world.

'I know, hard to believe now,' Mum said, watching my reaction through the rear-view mirror. 'The summers used to be so hot and dry that the grass would go all yellowy brown and sharp.'

'Like the grass in England?'

'Exactly like the grass in England now, poppet.' She turned her eyes back to the busy road and turned the radio on. Commentary about the local ice hockey league filled the silence.

For the rest of the car ride, I didn't say a word, too lost in my own thoughts. A question kept circulating in my mind.

Why had the world changed completely overnight?

AOIFE NILAND (she/her) is a writer based in Melbourne's west with an avid interest in exploring fantastical and supernatural concepts in a contemporary setting. She adores researching the history, folklore and myths of countries all around the world.

From Coast to City

Jasmine Claire

When I made the decision to move to the city, I cried for two weeks straight. I would curl up on the sand, tucked between two boat shacks so I couldn't be seen, look out at the water and let the tears fall down my face.

My first night in Melbourne I laid awake tossing and turning; the sound of traffic, sirens and general drunken rowdiness echoed in the streets outside. Back home the only sound was that of crashing waves, the streets deserted as soon as darkness fell. At one point, I gave up on sleep and I peered out my bedroom window. The city was alive with luminous light and bustling foot traffic; there was an exciting energy radiating from below. Above, three faint stars struggled to glow in the heavy black sky, so unlike the vast Milky Way visible back home.

I stared at the three stars, reasoning with myself. I wanted a life of purpose; I wanted the busy atmosphere the city provided. I couldn't live in fear forever. I allowed my goals to comfort me back to sleep.

Anxious to explore, I set out at first light. Early risers walking their dogs and heading to work passed by me; no acknowledgements or good mornings. The friendly smile I'd plastered on my face was lost on them. I tried not to take it personally, but it deterred me enough to stop trying.

The tram arrived late and people shuffled on impatiently. Inside, it was eerily silent of voices; no-one spoke, no-one looked at each other. Most people wore over-the-ear headphones with either a phone or book holding their attention.

An elderly woman got on two stops later but all seats were taken, so she stood awkwardly huddled against the rail.

'Would you like a seat?' I offered.

'Thank you, dear.' She gently patted my shoulder before moving to sit down.

I couldn't help comparing everything to the coast. When I took the bus people were more considerate, giving up their seats for those in need, saying hello and thank you to the bus driver. I feared not having that kind of community; the idea felt lonely and cold.

Born and raised by the bay, I was a coastal girl through and through. I never thought I could leave; the beach was my home, the sand and the water the only thing that had ever provided me with peace. But it came at a cost of a dead-end life. I wanted to chase a successful career in graphic design and the only way to achieve that was to escape the restrictive town. But in doing so, it meant leaving my mum all on her own, moving away from the only friends I'd ever known and starting my life over again. The change terrified me.

Through the tram doors I watched the world pass. It was a crisp morning in the city, every walking person was accompanied by a cup of coffee; some left behind a trail of white smoke in their striding wake. Nicotine and coffee, the standard city breakfast. How long would it take for me to pick up the habit?

A lanky man with opaque skin, face marked with scabbed spots, and holes in his grey tracksuit pants shuffled onto the tram. He wore a nice overcoat and carried a large hardback under his arm. The surrounding people glanced at him with apprehension. I observed him warily. He propped open his book and began to read an Arthurian legend aloud. Everyone turned around in utter surprise. He spoke so articulately, with so much old-timey characterisation that the carriage began to laugh, taking off their headphones to enjoy his spoken performance. I was enraptured, hanging off every captivating word. Upon arriving at his stop, he closed the book with a small thud, taking a bow as those around him appraised him for the morning entertainment. I exited the tram a few stops later with a smile on my face; the courage of the man was contagious.

In search of a quiet cafe to plan my day, I came across a quaint little nook tucked down a side alley. It appeared to be a go-to spot for work and study, a place I could sit and happily sketch designs in. The few people who were occupying tables each had a coffee, croissant and open laptop in front of them. The barista greeted me warmly.

'What can I get for you, hon?'

I was about to supply my usual order of a chai when I stopped myself. I never drank coffee, finding the taste too bitter and pungent. But I was in the city now, renowned for its incredible coffee. I might as well commit to the change to evolve into one of the city folk.

'I'll have a latte, but is there any way to make it not taste like coffee?'

She laughed warmly, 'Of course, I'll look after you.'

Over the noise of the steamer, the barista started a conversation with me. I confessed to her that I'd just moved to the city and knew no one. She nodded and responded, 'I moved six months ago from Perth, so I know how big of an adjustment it is. But now that I've lived here, I can't imagine ever going back.'

She shared the must-see places in the heart of the CBD; the National Gallery of Victoria, Queen Victoria Market and the Royal Botanic Gardens were the highlights of what she had explored for herself months ago. We talked for a while, the prepared coffee sitting forgotten between us on the counter.

'If you ever want someone to show you around, here's my mobile,' she offered.

A wave of gratitude washed over me, and I instantly felt lighter. My first friend in the city achieved on day one. My loneliness dissipated as excitement bubbled in my stomach.

I took a sip of my coffee; the smooth creamy drink had the perfect amount of sweetness to mask the bitterness. I could certainly get used to this.

Maybe the change wasn't all bad, the move from the coast to the city not as scary as I'd thought. I felt proud of my courage in pursuing a deeper purpose. There was no turning back from the path I'd embarked on and with each step it was feeling easier to embrace the unknown.

JASMINE CLAIRE (she/her) is a bookseller, writer and editor. Hailing from Naarm, you'll often find her at the park with a book and journal in hand. She's currently working on the manuscript of her sapphic, coming-of-age, skateboarding novel. Find her @jazz_claire1 (Instagram).

Hollow Faces

Marnie Rutland

They say when you miss someone, you start seeing them everywhere. Seeing their face on strangers in the street, the back of their head when they're not there, voices starting to mimic theirs until you're not sure what they sound like anymore.

Vivienne started to see her own face on other people. Not her now, her then. The Vivienne from five years ago. The perfect Vivienne. Sometimes they had the blonde hair she used to have, sometimes the brown she has now, other times neither. It was something about their facial features: big eyes, crooked nose, high cheekbones, slim lips. And yet it was nothing she could really put her finger on. Not enough to articulate properly.

Every time things reverted to normal, just when Vivienne would begin to forget, she'd see her face again. And she couldn't look away. Haunted. Like she was looking into a mirror and seeing the better version of herself. The version she couldn't seem to get back to, regardless of her efforts. At first, it had made her feel a weird kind of nostalgic, an ache in her heart for what was lost. Then she began to resent it, resent these strangers for something she couldn't even explain to herself. For having what she no longer wanted, like some cruel kind of deja vu.

Lately, however, the faces have changed. They've become harsher: their cheekbones sharper, eyes more sunken and jawlines unnaturally pronounced.

Vivienne notices this as she stares into one of those faces on the train home from the city. She left late today and so, by missing peak hour, she finds herself in a carriage empty but for her and the girl. She watches the girl closely, unsettled.

At first, it's like seeing a face that reminds you uncannily of a loved one. Vivienne can't tear her eyes away. The girl's face is tilted slightly down as she reads a book. But then things start to change. As the girl lifts her head, Vivienne notices the way her cheeks carve her face. She notices the dark circles that crease her face, shadowing around her eyes. Then something peculiar happens: the girl meets her eyes.

Usually, Vivienne wonders if the girl she's staring down even notices, or if they do, if they're as scared of her as she is of them. But they never look at her.

This girl holds eye contact. Vivienne feels entirely exposed, like she's been cut open for everyone to see.

Vivienne looks to the window beside her to focus on anything else, but instead she finds the reflected train carriage. The girl watches her through the reflection, but her features have altered: they're more withered, sunken, all skin and bone. Yet that's not what unsettles Vivienne most. What sends a cold rush of fear scratching through her veins is the blank face, the lack of recognition. The girl is looking right at her, yet right through her.

The automated voice announces the next station, and soon the train is stilling at the platform. But no-one gets on.

Vivienne glances about, only for her eyes to fall back on the girl, her head tilted back down, reading. She looks behind her down the carriage, finding it still empty.

When Vivienne turns back, the girl is standing right there, looming over her.

Vivienne looks up to find her face looking back at her. Her old face, eyes hard, circles around them and cheeks hollowed. Sickly, that's how she sees it now: a sickness of the mind personified.

She realises, with a start, that she's seeing the old Vivienne in a new light. Enough time has passed, and enough space has grown to fill it. That's what this is.

For truthfully, the old Vivienne wasn't perfect. The old her only looked that way. Really, she was the worst version of her. The one that thought terribly of everyone. The girl who was willing to carve out her own heart if it made her appear perfect.

The girl with Vivienne's face speaks. Her voice comes out thin and raspy. 'I've been looking for you, you know?'

'What?' Vivienne breathes.

'You stole my face.'

The girl reaches for Vivienne, nails digging into her wrist and tugging. Vivienne is up before she can process what's happening, yanking her wrist back, moving down the aisle towards the door between carriages. She can hear the girl's footsteps following her as she goes.

'You stole my face,' the girl calls after Vivienne, 'and I. Want. It. Back.' Her voice is a rasping whisper, like it pains her to breathe, let alone speak. Vivienne glances over her shoulder to see the girl moving faster towards her now.

Vivienne bolts for the door, pushing into the next carriage, the girl clawing after her. Then she's in the next carriage, reaching for the door to the carriage after that.

The girl is clawing after her, scraping her skin, trying and failing to find purchase. Her heavy breaths echo in Vivienne's head like scraping metal. In and out, in and out, in and out.

And then one of Vivienne's shoes catches on the floor. She slams to the ground.

The girl is on her in a moment and the two scramble for the upper hand, eyes catching. Vivienne struggles to stop the girl with her face from taking her life.

In the end, it's the girl's hand that catches Vivienne's, but it's Vivienne's hand that finds the back of the girl's head.

With a thump, the girl's face hits the train carriage floor. Again and again and again.

Vivienne stands alone in the carriage, just her and what was the girl.

Now the face she sees before her is not hers anymore.

The face she sees is bloody.

The face she sees is hollow.

The face she sees is yours.

MARNIE RUTLAND (she/her) is an aspiring fiction writer. She writes mostly thrillers and crime fiction, dipping her toes into romance and horror elements. Marnie has a passion for fashion and is inspired by the use of suspense in Hitchcock films and the like.

A New Home

Vicki Papa

This is an excerpt from a larger work,
The Incredible Adventures of Fred.

I stuck my head out of the window that Mr Archie had left open for me.

'Here we are, Fred.'

We were really here! We were in front of Mr Archie's house. After Mrs Margaret passed away and I was taken away, I never thought I'd see this place again. He rescued me from that awful pet 'resort' (aka jail). How could I ever thank him? Ever repay him?

Mr Archie jumped out of the driver's seat and opened the door to unbuckle me. I was free. I had an open door to his front yard and I could go anywhere! But I was frozen in my seat.

'Don't you want to come in?' Mr Archie sounded worried, and I didn't want him to.

I didn't want Mr Archie to think I wasn't excited about being rescued, so I leaped out of the car like a gymnast. But in my haste to impress Mr Archie, I hadn't considered the rain from the last couple of days, and I landed in the middle of a muddy puddle. Eek! I shook the wet dirt off me and studied my surroundings. My tail wouldn't stop wagging and I didn't know where to go or what to look at first. I had marked my territory under his lemon tree (Mr Archie never tells me off), under the lavender bush and even by Mrs Archie's rose bushes when she wasn't looking. They smelt amazing, and I wasn't about to let any of the neighbourhood cats stake their claim on them. This was my hood.

But then I remembered Mrs Margaret. I ran to the front of the driveway and looked out onto Mrs Margaret's old house next door, my old house. Mr Archie didn't run after me. I loved him for that. He allowed me my time. My tail suddenly stopped wagging and became lifeless. Mr Archie leaned over the white picket fence, 'I know, Fred. I miss her too.'

It was weird looking at Mrs Margaret's house as an outsider. Without her there, it looked bare. The blinds were drawn shut and weeds had started to grow in the garden bed. Mrs Margaret would never have let any weeds grow. Although I missed Mrs Margaret terribly, the place looked foreign now. I didn't want to be there if she was no longer around. My home was next door now, with Mr and Mrs Archie. So, I walked back around into Mr Archie's driveway. He crouched down and gave me a pat, stroking my fur from my neck all the way to the top of my tail.

'Wow' he said. 'Weren't they feeding you in that place?'

No! I wanted to tell him. They were not! I was in a five-star pet resort and they were feeding me food out of a can. They thought I was stupid. I was supposed to be getting gourmet pet food cooked by a top chef. The brochures had showed juicy prime rib steaks dripping with lamb fat and roast chicken and potato swimming in a pool of gravy. 'Nothing but the best!' was their slogan. Yeah right. I knew it wasn't freshly cooked, and there was no way I was eating that crap. I wouldn't stand for it; the injustice of it. So, I went on a hunger-strike. Mrs Margaret had entrusted me to them. She'd done her research, *meticulously.* She wanted the best for me after she left this earth. I know her heart was in the right place, but little did she know what was happening behind closed doors.

They were supposed to be taking me out for walks three times a day. How many times did they take me out? Not once! They had a pool for swimming and sun baking, not that I would've liked it. I *hate* the water. But still, that's not the point. How many times did I go swimming? Zero. They had an agility and obstacle course. How many times did they take me there? Zero. They had a sandpit for digging. Guess how many times they took me there? Zero.

I spent all my time locked up in a five by one metre enclosure, on a bed that had been slept on by at least ten other dogs, being fed *canned* food, and in the company of another twenty dogs in the enclosures next to me, barking all day and all night. They just wouldn't shut up. They were not my friends. I didn't want to be near any of them.

Mr Archie stood. 'Come on, let's get you something to eat.' That was music to my ears. At my darkest moments, it was the thought of Mr and Mrs Archie's delicious lemon and herb-spiced lamb chops that saved me.

He unlocked the front door and opened it. From inside wafted Mrs Archie's cooking: lentils. It must be a Friday. Mrs Archie tended to cook lentils on Fridays, and I realised I wouldn't be getting anything delicious like lamb chops on a Friday. But after the rubbish they'd tried to feed me over the last few months, I'd eat Mrs Archie's lentils any day, especially since they didn't come out of a can.

Mrs Archie barely looked at me when I came in. Didn't she want me here? I hadn't ever considered that. Had she seen me pee next to her rose bushes?

'I don't think Fred can eat lentils since you put onions in there,' Mr Archie said.

I'll have the lentils! I'll have the lentils! I barked, trying to get his attention, trying to tell him that Mrs Archie's lentils would be just fine.

Mrs Archie lifted the lid from the saucepan and dipped a teaspoon into her soup, 'Mmm, yep. Just perfect,' she said.

She replaced the lid and wiped her hands over the floral apron she wore. Then turned around and put her hands on her hips, looked down at me and frowned.

My heart sank and I lowered my head to the ground, resting it on top of my front two paws. Was she angry with me?

She then opened the fridge, and I looked up. She rummaged through a bag and pulled out... a bone. A *bone*!

VICKI PAPA (she/her) writes fiction for both teens and adults across several genres including contemporary romance and historical fiction. Visit vickipapa.com to say hello and find out more about her work.

The Panic of Time

Gemma Catarina

I find it hard to recall memories from my childhood. It's like looking through a foggy window and trying to find happiness in the smeared shadows. My five-year-old self knocks at the window, staring for attention. Looking at her, at this girl that was once full of excitement, pure love and innocence, my tear ducts well up from jealousy. I wrap my arms around myself for comfort, but she runs to hug my legs tightly, letting me know – she's still here.

><><

Sundays were my favourite. 8:30 am mass with Mum, followed by breakfast and shopping. It was a routine, and I liked routines. I'd say the same prayer each time, and it had to be the exact same or else I'd start over. It always began with sending my love to the deceased and listing names in the same order. The names were foreign, distant relatives I didn't know. Eventually the list became too long, and guilt trapped me when I was more concerned about not remembering the exact order of names rather than the deceased. Although my time in church was spent shooing away intrusive thoughts and itching at the incorrect order of names, I was happy to be out of the house with Mum. We both loved being away for as long as we could. Home only felt like home when it was just us and my brother; with Dad around, it was more like a *house*.

Family gatherings always brought on a stomach-ache. It's always a weird feeling when you're surrounded by people, but you still feel alone. I like to think I've learned to welcome that weird feeling: learning to accept my own quietness, to not feel awkward silences, to only select the kind words that come out of people's mouths. I've learned the art of listening; it comes in handy.

In prep, I pinky promised my classmate that I'd never share her secrets. At fifteen, I promised my best friend I'd never tell her parents she smoked. More than once, I swore to Mum I'd never tell Dad. The pinky-wrapped giggles had turned into vows of unspoken regards, a child holding words only an adult should know. The longer I held on, the harder it was to let go.

On my sixteenth birthday, I smiled to the melody of 'Happy birthday', yet all I could focus on was time escaping me, rising away like the smoke from the candles. I couldn't really tell how much had changed from my last birthday or the one before, except I was a few centimetres taller. My mind felt disconnected to the physical cage I was in. As a child, I yearned to be older, but now that I finally was, it all felt wrong. Change felt forced upon me. My twelve-year-old self would be thrilled that she was finally a cool teenager, good for her, but I didn't feel comfortable in this body. My training bra was replaced with a C-cup, and now I had to check that my school dress buttons weren't gaping open. I was either a *child* or an *adult*, being told to shut up or speak up. I felt desperate to hold onto my childhood that I was leaving behind.

It was all happening too quickly.

⨯⨯⨯

The panic of time has felt heavy in my chest since I was a little girl. There's this pressure that haunts me, to constantly be and do better, to change, to adapt, to transform. The ticking of the second hand pairs with the beating inside. I dream of feeling a release. I hate how quickly time escapes and I hate that I can't hold onto its hands for longer. It's always been a wish of mine to go back in time. What would I do over? How could I make things different? *Could* I make things different?

If I had the chance, I'd use that wish to be a child again – to be allowed to be one.

><><

I'm now twenty years old, standing with my feet in the grass, prickles catching beneath – prickles of promises, memories and time. I've decided to begin my twenties acknowledging all parts of myself. My inner child *and* teenage self. I won't let them be forgotten and I won't let my adult self feel unworthy. Living with unwanted change is something I'm learning to accept, so I'll hold my own hand and walk through it gently. For my next birthday, I'm not sure what I'll wish for. I just hope to feel the same as the number of candles that are placed in front of me.

So, cheers to the unknown. I clink my glass with a head full of thoughts that'll forever be left wandering, and the overflowing bubbles spill away with my past emotions. As I take a sip, the crisp refreshment tastes like a clean start to life. I've learned that I can't change my childhood and that's okay: I don't want to anymore. There's no need to carry the burden of worry, to be jealous of the past and desperate about the future.

><><

I see my five-year-old self at the window. Instead of staying with her, I tell her it's all going to be okay. I let go and leave her be.

GEMMA CATARINA (she/her) has a heart full of passion for all things literature, especially for young-adult fiction, romance and poetry. She's eager to explore the world of writing and pursue her interest in editing after graduating. Visit @gemcatwriting (Instagram).

Cut From a Certain Cloth

Sarah Rosina Winkler

The tiles are cold against my feet
as I step onto the scale for the first time in years,
bracing myself to be weighed in the balance
and found wanting.
I remind myself that
just because they're the only things that count,
numbers do not mean anything.
When I was younger, I would secretly admire the curve of my neck
and the sunlight hitting my skin
and the light lighting up my eyes,
in the rear-view mirror,
from the back seat of the car.
I never told anyone
because ugly girls aren't allowed to think
they're anything but ugly.
It has taken so long for me to like my silhouette
more than only in my shadow
when the sun is to my back.
My mother used to make me a dress every birthday,
but they went mainly unworn
because I felt they were too beautiful for my body
and instead chose clothes that covered my form.

Nowadays, we plan the clothes she makes for me together
as she thinks I might wear them
if I have a say in the conversation
around their creation,
and she knows I must love the body
I have grown into.
So the clothes I choose
are big
and bold
and bright to please the eyes
and made of flattering fabrics.
But still my crop tops hang untouched in my wardrobe,
the door of which is a sliding mirror
that exposes around my navel the angry red lines
like fingertips brushing against condensed glass;
at first, I thought they were scars
from where I'd scratched the itch
of too-tight waistbands pressing in on me,
but in truth, these are the marks on my skin
from where my skin stretched thin
– the combination of stress
and medication to cope with that stress
and stress-eating
making its mark on me.
I can tolerate my shape,
stop comparing myself
because I am myself,
not someone else,

but I step down from the scale
feeling devalued by the value given.
I pause to once more accept my corporeal being
being what it has become
before writing down the number for the doctor.

SARAH ROSINA WINKLER (she/they) is a writer and editor of creative non-fiction, long-form fiction, poetry and more. Sarah's writing, informed by political sensibilities that developed at an early age, often touches on mental health, neurodivergence and queer awareness. In their spare time, they read young-adult literature and listen to audio fiction podcasts.

The Guest

Julie Faulkner

They had been friends for decades, the older woman and the younger woman – the guest. Living in neighbouring suburbs made it easy to accept the younger woman's invitations to stay for dinner or swim in the pool on a hot day. Their daughters were close and so their lives connected around school life. The older woman could arrive at the younger woman's house with a salad, drink her wine and leave after a few hours. Together, the women would commiserate over difficult children, insensitive husbands or new ways with chicken. But once home, the older woman would mock the raucous laughter and pick over the ridiculous things the younger woman had said.

It was when the younger woman and her husband moved away that boundaries began to blur. The younger woman often needed a place to stay when she returned to the city and assumed the older woman would have no objection. A welcome was expected when the younger woman suggested she visit annually for their shared April birthdays.

The younger woman was always insisting the older woman stay with her, which she had found to be a claustrophobic experience. The older woman wearied of trying to steer the conversation away from incessant preoccupations – ailments (there were many), grateful or ungrateful children, gossip or pets. The younger woman and her husband often fought, and after each fight she would complain about him to the older woman. The younger woman did not work or read or even watch television, so there were few opportunities to escape her prattle. Soon, the older woman became curt and uncharitable in her responses, yet her rudeness was no deterrent. Although she had never extended an invitation to the younger woman, the older woman realised she had also done nothing to discourage her from staying.

And so, the older woman sought advice from mutual friends. One friend temporarily distracted the younger woman and another offered alternative accommodation. But there was always a reason why the younger woman should not or could not stay with them – the cat set off her allergies or the hosts had their family staying. Another friend argued that the older woman was enabling the bad behaviour by not dealing with the younger woman directly. Maybe she was, but had too many years passed for the older woman to suddenly become a different person in the younger woman's eyes?

Each year, the visits south grew longer and on one visit the younger woman and her husband had extended their stay from three to five to seven days. On the fifth day, the younger woman announced she would remain for the week, which prompted the older woman to set some ground rules. Surely that would not threaten the relationship. However, the younger woman had once again fought with her husband and he had left with suitcase in hand. The younger woman was enraged by the abrupt departure, and so the older woman felt it best to say nothing that might further disturb her guest.

The following night, the older woman was suffering from a painfully stiff neck. After dinner, the younger woman offered to massage her neck and suggested her host take two magnesium tablets as muscle relaxants. Temporarily relieved, the older woman went to bed, found an angle to rest her head, and fell asleep.

The younger woman had asked the older woman to take her shopping and she had reluctantly agreed. The older woman woke the next morning feeling queasy and weak so cancelled her plans to take the younger woman out, delegating the task to a friend. The dizziness did not subside during the day. When the older woman went to use her bathroom in the late afternoon, she found the younger woman in her shower; she explained that she had forgotten her shampoo and hoped her host did not mind her using hers. The older woman grabbed hold of the bathroom cabinet, said nothing, and returned to bed.

The older woman had intended to leave for an interstate trip at the end of the week with her son coming to pet sit. But as she lay in bed, she heard the younger woman on the phone, 'No that's okay, no need to come. I'll look after the dogs.'

The older woman struggled to lift her shoulders and head from the sheets. Inwardly she screamed, but she could only utter a few spluttered sounds. She felt nauseous and trapped. Where was her husband? She could not remember. Not even the dogs had entered her room to see her. Her friends were not answering her messages. The younger woman appeared, bearing a tray of toast, tea and curatives. The older woman wanted to tell her to get out of her house, to leave her alone, but in her weakened state, she could do nothing more than lie where she was.

Whenever the older woman dredged herself from her dozy state, the younger woman was sitting by her bed, staring at her.

'You'll be alright,' assured the younger woman, unblinking. 'You'll be fine.'

She lowered the grey blind.

The older woman was exhausted, no longer able to move.

The afternoon wore on and in the sallow fading light, the older woman watched as a fly buzzed in vain against the window.

JULIE FAULKNER (she/her) was an English teacher and teacher educator in a previous life. A reading enthusiast, she's judged the Picture Book Award for the Children's Book Council of Australia (CBCA) and co-edited a literacy journal for teachers. As a learner, editor and Italiophile, she values opportunities to challenge and expand her communicative repertoire. Find out more @joolsforkz15 (Instagram).

One of Them

Katy Addis

This is an excerpt from a larger work,
Staring at Stalin.

It would have looked like any other Ukrainian sitting room –
with a wood heater, two faded brown armchairs and a full
bookshelf – except for the desk covered in papers and the
portrait of Stalin hanging above it. It was the same portrait
that hung in Tomasz's classroom. He shuddered.

Sitting behind the desk was a woman, tall and thin with
pale-blue glassy eyes and hair pulled back into a tight bun. Her
Soviet uniform was ironed into sharp creases and pointy ends.
She looked up and frowned.

The man who'd brought him here pushed him forward.
'Tomasz Nowak for you, comrade.'

'Him?' she said, her eyebrows slightly raised. 'He's tiny.'

'Fourteen years old,' said the man.

Tomasz's head started to spin. Just ten minutes ago he'd been
walking home from school, minding his own business. A strange
man had taken his arm, called him by name and warned him
not to shout as he'd steered him into this house. They knew his
name and age. What else did they know? Did they know his
father was German? His knees started to shake.

'Thank you, comrade,' said the lady. 'I'll take it from
here.' She pointed to a chair next to the desk, then beckoned
Tomasz. 'Sit.'

Tomasz sat, holding his shaking legs down with his hands.

Picking up a piece of paper, she read aloud, 'Tomasz Nowak. Fourteen years old.' Her mouth pursed. 'Father applied for the family to be repatriated to Germany in 1940 but was refused. Grounds unknown. Oh dear.' She paused and glanced up at Tomasz. 'How unfortunate.'

They knew. His hands began to tremble. He sat on them.

'Don't worry,' she said, with a smile that didn't reach her eyes. 'This presents an opportunity for you, does it not?'

Tomasz didn't answer. His mind was furiously whirring. He had to keep his wits about him, work out what was happening. He had to do whatever he could to keep his family safe, keep Anna safe.

'Now,' she said, pushing a piece of paper and a pen towards him. 'You will write: I, Tomasz Nowak, undertake to work for the NKGB to supply regular information.'

His mouth fell open. They wanted him to spy for the Soviet secret police. That's what they'd brought him here for.

He looked down at the blank paper, which lay waiting for his traitorous words. The pen shook as he picked it up. He lowered it to the paper, but his hand froze. *Think, Tomasz, think. You have to get out of this somehow.*

The lady tapped her fingers on the desk. 'Start writing.' In a louder voice, she repeated, 'I, Tomasz Nowak, undertake to work for the NKGB to supply regular information.'

'I think... there must be some sort of mistake,' he said, looking up at her. 'I'm— I'm just a child. I don't understand.'

She sighed. 'Not a child, a young man with a German father. You are now to work for us. Just write what I said.'

Tomasz laid the pen down. 'You want me to be a spy?' His voice came out all squeaky.

The lady leaned forwards, her eyes unreadable. 'Listen carefully. Your job will be to tell us if anyone at your school says anything bad about Stalin. You will supply us with information.'

'You want me to inform on my classmates?' He couldn't believe what he was hearing. They were getting children to spy now?

'Not only classmates,' she said coolly. 'Teachers too.'

Tomasz's stomach lurched. He was supposed to spy on adults as well? He had to find a way out of this and fast. *Think, Tomasz, think.*

'They don't like me, the other kids.' He stared at the floor as he spoke. 'They don't talk to me. I'm— I'm very shy. And people never say anything bad about Stalin. Not at our school. We—' His throat constricted. 'We all love Stalin. I'd be useless as an informer. I think someone else would be better.'

He shrank down. If he could disappear into the chair, he would. The clock on the wall ticked loudly, and Tomasz forced himself to breathe. *Please just let me go. Please.*

The lady stood up and walked around to his side of the desk. She picked up his hand and placed the pen in it. Then she leaned down and spoke into his ear. The feel of her breath made him squirm.

'Listen to me, Tomasz. If you don't sign this form, the police will be at your house tonight to arrest your father. Not only him; the whole family... including your little sister. What's her name again?' She paused. 'That's right... Anna.'

He felt bile rising in his stomach. They would take Anna.

'Now do you understand?' said the lady, straightening up.

His brain stopped whirring, and it suddenly all became clear. He had no choice. This wasn't about him choosing to be brave and refusing to sign. He couldn't get out of this by being clever either. If he didn't sign, they'd arrest his family. It was as simple as that. He was completely and utterly powerless.

He lowered the pen to the paper, took several deep breaths and started writing.

I, Tomasz Nowak, undertake to work for the NKGB to supply regular information.

The lady smiled. 'I'm glad you signed it.' She reached over and took the paper away, checking what he'd written. 'Now,' she said, looking at him, 'you're not to tell anyone about this. Not your family, not anyone. We'll be in touch.' She motioned to the door. 'You can make your own way out.'

Tomasz rose unsteadily, opened the door and walked up the corridor, holding the wall to support his shaking legs. Once he was outside, he sat on the curb and vomited until there was nothing left inside him.

Half an hour ago he was just a schoolboy. Now he was one of them.

KATY ADDIS (she/her) is a writer, musician and teacher who loves writing for and working with young people. She's travelled around Australia presenting school shows with her comedy duo Brass Bedlam. In 2020, Katy was shortlisted for the Children's Book Council of Australia (CBCA) Maurice Saxby Creative Development Program for two of her picture books. Email kaddis@melbpc.org.au to get in touch.

There's This Thing Called the Internet

Belinda Coleman

'There's this thing called the internet. You might have heard of it.'

The kid guffaws at his own joke, slapping his hand on the table in front of him.

The older man opposite puts his beer down, wondering for the sixth time in two minutes why he agreed to let this whippersnapper share the table.

It had started with a small comment from the older man about the burning sun and the need for an umbrella. 'Didn't think to check the weather?' the kid prodded. 'Too old to know about the weather app?' To the kid, this apparently meant the older man was also too old to know about the internet.

There would be few alive who *didn't* know what the internet was, but still, this kid – a greasy haired, gangly specimen – thought he was funny. The older man watches as the kid shoves a plastic straw into the tin can of a diet coke – never mind that he's been given a glass with ice – and slurps. Loudly. He checks his watch, noting it had only been forty-five seconds since he last looked.

Another nail-on-chalkboard slurp. Another glance at the watch followed by an almost imperceptible shift in the older man's face, a tightening of the wrinkled skin around his eyes and a slight arching of a grey eyebrow. His spry, wrinkled finger brushes across the dawdling watch face, removing a speck of dust that is visible only to him. He glances up, purses his lips and considers the gangly youth in front of him before coming to a decision and settling into a hunched position. *Let's give him old.*

'Tell me about this intro-net.' He mangles the pronunciation, extending the *i*, slurring the *e*, probably overdoing it.

But apparently not – the kid seems happy to assume him ignorant and lets out his squawking cackle of a laugh again, almost choking on his drink.

'It's in*ter*net.'

He laughs. Perhaps it's all he does.

'Boy, I knew this area was a backwater, but really!'

It isn't a backwater and the internet connection is fine. There are a few trees left, unlike the city blocks where every tree is removed to make way for cookie-cutter houses. Each one as boring and unoriginal as the last, but that doesn't make it a backwater.

'Please explain this internet.'

One of the serving girls smirks as she passes the table and gives the older man a knowing nod. The kid's forehead puckers as he tries to compose some sort of response to the question. *Perhaps he should Google it.*

'The internet is…' He falters, shrugging.

Honestly, he can't get more than that?

'Yes?' the older man prods, spreading his hands in an inviting gesture.

'The internet is a thing that… tells you things.'

'Really?'

'Yes.'

He sounds more confident now, though who knows why. 'What things?'

'Well, umm. Everything.'

'So, this internet can tell me what I ate for breakfast?'

'Well, no.'

'No?'

He's fidgeting with the glass now. Drink from the can, play with the glass. Interesting. Maybe he learnt it on the internet. 'It tells you other things. Like what the weather is going to be or what's happening in the news.'

'So it's like a radio.'

This kid probably hasn't even seen a radio before.

'I mean, sure, but you, like, ask it questions.'

'So, I can talk to this internet, and it can tell me things?'

'Well, yeah, sometimes. You can use Google to write to it, or you can use Siri to—'

'I'm sorry, I don't understand what you're asking. Could you repeat that?' Siri pipes up. For the first time the kid notices a smartphone sitting on the table next to the older man's elbow.

His flushed face creases as he tries to figure out what's going on.

'You have an iPhone?' he asks at last.

'Yes.'

'But surely it uses the internet,' he says, staring in confusion.

The old man holds the boy's gaze. 'What if I told you I invented the internet?'

The kid's laugh explodes in an incredulous squark. 'As if!'

'Back in the 1970s I was part of a team in the US army who worked on the ARPANET. We set up a computer right here actually—' he gestures to the beer garden around them, 'and we ran cables to a van in the carpark. We made the first wireless transmission from one computer to another – one network to another. Here, to Menlo Park, and a day later to Boston.'

His weathered face breaks into a slight smile as he surveys the beer garden, still very much unchanged from that day. But the excitement. That he can still remember. The energy, the facial expressions when it actually worked. Beer had never tasted better than when they poured it on that afternoon to celebrate the victory.

'Then it grew,' the older man continued, 'The ARPANET became the internet, and – clearly – spread far wider than the US army.'

Of course, the Alpine Inn had only been one small, but vital piece in a much bigger chain of events. It was only looking back much later that they realised they had made the pivotal breakthrough right here, in this obscure beer garden.

The waitress approaches with the older man's meal.

'Sir, your alpine burger.' She tries unsuccessfully to hide her amusement as she puts down the plate.

'Thank you, Sally,' he replies then turns back to the kid whose mouth is hanging open.

The kid finally finds his voice. 'You can't be serious.'

'Oh, I'm serious.'

'You invented the internet…' he looks around as though he's misplaced something, then finishes lamely, 'here—in the middle of nowhere.'

'Well actually, it was from that picnic table over there. But yes, here at the Alpine Inn.'

He's still gawking.

The older man looks him in the eye, silently thanking the kid for the entertaining story to tell his granddaughter tonight, 'There's this thing called the internet. Google it.'

BELINDA COLEMAN (she/her) is a Melbourne-based writer and editor who's currently working on her first novel. She loves to read a good classic or fantasy, but her favourite genre is historical fiction. Find out more @belindacolementwrites (Instagram) and Belinda Coleman Writes (Facebook).

The Inventigators

Amy Adeney

This is an excerpt from a larger work of junior fiction, *The Inventigators: a squawking solution*.

The Inventigators didn't happen all at once. It happened a bit at a time, like ingredients going into a delicious recipe.

Nina and Joe have lived next door to me forever, and since we're in the same grade at school, we've always seen a lot of each other. First they were just my neighbours, then my friends, and pretty soon after that we were besties. So, a couple of years ago, after only four months of nonstop begging, our parents agreed to put a gate in the fence that separated our backyards. Looking back, I guess that was when it all began.

It was Nina's idea to take over the shed in my backyard. We spent a whole weekend un-cobwebbing it and stacking all my parents' stuff in the corner. When we were done, Nina turned the workbench into her laboratory – she's the scientist of our group. She has her own chemistry set, a microscope, a lab coat and safety glasses. Pretty professional.

Then Joe said if Nina gets to do her thing in the shed, he should get to do his thing too. Twins are like that sometimes. So, the art easel was set up in the middle of the shed, and Joe brought in a whole box of paints and paper and brushes and other stuff to make his creations. He'd never admit it, but he's super talented. He even got to paint a mural on the tuckshop wall at our school. It made perfect sense that he should have his own studio.

And since the shed is in *my* backyard, Nina said, 'Dash, you really should have your own spot in here too.'

We found a dusty old couch that someone had left on the side of the road and carried it all the way home by ourselves. It *just* fit across the back of the shed. Then Dad knocked me up some bookshelves – sometimes having a builder for a dad is pretty handy. I brought out lots and lots of books (but left lots and lots in my bedroom too) and set up my library. See, I'm kind of a whiz at history and facts.

Once our shed was a library, a laboratory and a studio, it wasn't too long before it became known as the Libratorio. None of us can remember who came up with the name first, but I'm pretty sure it was me. Don't tell Nina – she likes it when things are her idea.

Anyway, if you have a clubhouse, you pretty much have to become a club. So, we took Nina's science and Joe's art and my reading, and we became the Inventigators. It's not like we're superheroes or anything. We don't have special powers, we don't go on missions and we certainly don't wear capes. We just notice things that need fixing and we try to fix them.

So, if you have a problem that needs some scientific, bookish, arty inventing, now you know where to find us.

><><

As soon as Joe and Nina walk into the Libratorio on Monday morning, I can tell something's wrong. Usually, the school holidays mean smiles and relaxing and pizza for lunch. But Joe and Nina look miserable.

'Well that was just about the worst sleep I've ever had,' says Nina, flopping down on our dusty couch.

'Worst sleep,' agrees Joe, rubbing his eyes.

'I was just getting to a particularly interesting part of my dream – sharing a bowl of nachos with Albert Einstein. Then those outrageous birds started their noisy squawking and – *bang* – I'm wide awake. And it was still pitch-black outside! Even the sun doesn't wake up that early. And I'll never find out who got the last nacho...'

Looks like being tired makes Nina even more dramatic than usual.

'What birds?' I ask. I didn't hear any birds this morning. But then again, Mum and Dad often say that I could sleep through a cyclone.

'The noisy ones,' says Joe, which doesn't tell me anything I don't already know.

'The colourful ones. I'm pretty sure they're lorikeets,' says Nina. 'Ever since that empty block up the street became a giant building site, the birds that used to live there seem to have made their new home outside our bedroom windows. And if you think we're grouchy, you should see our dad!'

'So, what are we going to do about it?' I ask.

'There are many factors to consider,' begins Nina. 'Obviously we don't want to harm the birds or mess with their habitat. Unlike the local council, who doesn't seem to care if they destroy the birds' homes!'

'Just need them to move away from our windows,' says Joe.

I wander over to my bookshelf and run my finger across the rows, looking for my *Big Book of Birds*. There's no wi-fi in the Libratorio, so it's way quicker to look things up in books than to trek up to the house and use the internet. Joe has his thinking-face on: eyes closed, forehead wrinkled.

'We definitely have our work cut out for us,' says Nina.

Looks like these holidays won't be as relaxing as I expected. I guess we'd better make that pizza an extra large.

AMY ADENEY (she/her) is an experienced primary teacher, and the author of the junior fiction series *Tilda Teaches* (Five Mile) and the picture book *Turning Cartwheels* (EK Books). She has a second junior fiction series, *Trick Shot Trevor* (Five Mile), published in 2023. Her next picture book will be published by Affirm Press in 2024.

Minor Side Effects

Saskia Udvary

Wednesday

Everyone has said I will regret this. I beg to differ. The way I see it, I get free treatment and a holiday until I am better. That is what M, my doctor, said, adding that there may be minor side effects.

I want to document my experience, if not for anyone but myself. It will give me something to do with my spare time.

Right now I feel numb. But, in some ways, feeling numb is better than feeling sad.

Thursday

Yesterday was strange. I have noticed I do not have much of an appetite. M says I am not to worry and should have it back in a few days. Until then, I should rest.

Friday

I feel *something* is with me, but I do not know what. I am trying not to think about it, but I could hear it last night when I tried to sleep. A rustling in the walls. I carved a hole. There was nothing there, but I could still hear it. It only stopped when the sun came up.

I tried asking M, but he has gone away on holiday, and according to Z, the receptionist, 'M will not be back for quite some time'. Z told me that the rustling is normal and whatever it is will leave in time.

Saturday
This morning, I seemed to be covered in strange bites when I woke up. Later, when I went to the bathroom, I saw what had bitten me. They were coming from the drain. There were hordes of them. They were small, greyish-silver and hissed as I entered the room, so I shut the door and left them there. I will deal with them later when I felt better; perhaps they will be gone by then.

Sunday
Today, for the first time since I came here, I felt like eating something. I am starting to feel better. I have developed a craving for raw meat, which someone brought me this morning. It was blood red and smooth. It looked flavourful. I wondered if it was okay to eat.
I quite liked it.

Wednesday
I last entered the bathroom a few days ago. I did not want to disturb them, the bugs. But today, I began to worry about the state of the bathroom, so I asked for M. Instead, Z gave me a letter that M had written. It read: *I am in terrible danger, and so are you. Please disregard everything I have said. I am sorry – leave if you can.*

After I read it, Z asked for it back, which puzzled me. Apparently it is part of the treatment facility's protocol. It is essential to have only limited contact with others and the outside world to get the best out of the treatment.

A few hours later, Z called me. She informed me that M had abruptly quit and would not be returning, which means I have no doctor. This makes me incredibly anxious.

I asked Z about the bugs. She laughed and said I was not to worry, that it means the treatment is working.

Thursday

Today I finally went back into the bathroom. The bugs were nearly gone.

I asked Z if I might go outside for a short while and get some fresh air. I thought it might help ease my anxiety. She said no; she was very adamant about it. When I asked why, she gasped. She looked puzzled, her brow began to knit into an almost grotesque pattern, and the coffee cup she held began to shake. I found this profoundly troubling.

I am trying to figure out what to do. There seems to be no answers now that M is gone.

Saturday

I ended up calling Z again; she sent someone to my room to keep me company.

The lady's name is V. I asked her why M left. She explained that he had failed. I asked what that meant. She explained that M no longer believed in the treatment and that Z did not want people working for them who did not support their practices. I guess that makes sense.

Last night V was very professional. Tonight, however, V was acting strange. I can write now because she felt sick and went to sleep in the next room. She said that she could hear something in the walls, and that she was worried for her safety and mine. She confessed that she was not so sure about working here anymore, and she wished she had never come here for treatment. She said she did not believe that M quit, but that something else made him leave. She said I should try and leave while I still can.

I would have asked her more about it, but she needs to get better. It will have to wait until tomorrow.

Monday

V is dead. I found her Sunday morning. The bugs were crawling from her mouth. Z came to talk to me. She said V's death was her own fault because she no longer believed in their practices.

Z has given me a new medication, as I am nearing the end of my treatment. I guess she could see I was not doing so well, because she said that she was once in the same position as me and that, with time, I would begin to feel better, not just about myself but also about the treatment. I am not sure if I will write much more. I do not feel so good now.

Tuesday

I realised I have never written my name here. My name is L, and today I am better. So, I have decided to stay here and help. I have been assigned to a new patient, who I am meeting later today.

I know this will work out because, unlike M and V, I am not a failure. I have succeeded, unlike those who came before me.

SASKIA UDVARY (she/her) is a Melbourne-based short story writer of the horror and thriller genres. As well as women's roles in fiction, she writes about her favourite books, movies and TV shows. Email saskiauwriter@gmail.com or visit @saskiareadssometimes (Instagram) to get in touch.

A Dream

Jaidyn Kew

I open my eyes. For a split second I see a light – a bright, blinding light – then it's gone. I look around the dark abyss that surrounds me.

It's all darkness, nothing to see, nothing to touch, nothing.

A surge of emotions starts to well up within me, loneliness, regret, guilt and sadness. A sadness that soon envelops all my previous emotions, one that forces me to my knees, that brings me to tears, that convinces me to regret everything I've done up until this point, reminding me of a guilt that I feel can never be forgiven… one that brings me great loneliness.

I could feel it all oozing out of me. I should do something to stop it, but I can't, there's so much.

There's too much.

But, in my heart there's a faint glimmer, small but noticeable. It grows into a glowing orb, slowly moving to my dripping sadness, attempting to clear its impurities, then disappearing moments later.

Dark, muddy colour seeps back into this… mess.

As I kneel in my own puddle of emotions, letting it all move over and through me, I see the same light again in the distance. It shines just as brightly as before. After adjusting my eyes to it, I can make out some sort of figure.

A person, someone I know… a friend, slowly walking over towards me.

She sees me in my now pool of emotions all swirling around

me, murky and strangely sticky, like I'm in a vat of tar. She helps me stand up, careful to not let me slip or fall over.

'I'm happy to see you again,' she says with a smile.

Ashamed to even look at her, I look down, the darker parts now swirling around me becoming thicker, all amalgamating into one giant mess.

She keeps hold of me.

'Hey, it's okay, it's not your fault.'

Those words break me into tears. I can't hold them back. I start to feel all the regret and guilt well up inside of me, chaining me back down, sinking. With so much regret and guilt overflowing within me, I don't know what to do. I can only fall back down and silently cry while she stands in front of me.

She kneels down, making sure to be level with me. She tells me, 'It was never your fault, you did what you could and I'm proud of you.'

She lifts her warm, gentle hand, and softly presses it against my face.

'Just... don't make the same mistake I did, you can learn from me,' pausing momentarily to look away, she turns back to me. 'I don't want you to end up like me, you can still change things, I believe in you.'

I look up at her, her smiling, kind and forgiving face. There isn't a single trace of malice or ill will.

'I'm... sorry that I couldn't help you.' Tears still streaming from my face, dripping from my chin, creating ripples in the now uncontrollable mess.

'Don't be sorry, remember,' she lowers her hand to hold mine, 'it's not your fault. I'll say that as many times as I need to.'

I want to reject that... I want to express everything to her... but the words won't come out, just more noises of sobbing and heaving.

She leans in and wraps her arms around me.

'It's okay.'

I sense a small shift beneath me, it's slow... but I can feel that stickiness starting to let go. I feel that same glimmer surface and move through my loneliness, the pool at my feet slowly becoming clearer and smoother. It's still there... but it doesn't feel as heavy.

'I believe in you, even if you don't right now.'

She holds me closer.

'I can see that hope in you that will influence others, give them courage, give them strength and give them hope. Just... don't make the same mistake I did.'

She gently pats my head.

'I know you can do it, better than anyone.'

Even though I want to disagree with her... even though I know that I could have done something... I can't ignore her words. I can't ignore her true feelings.

All that regret and guilt that had been festering in me is now overshadowed with gratitude and compassion. Maybe it's hers. Maybe it's mine. Maybe a little bit of both.

I can still feel that pinching reminder of regret, mixed in there somewhere. But it's no longer chained to me.

I hold her tight, finally accepting her embrace, thanking her for everything she's done, for the hope that she's given me. No... the hope she has helped me realise.

'I won't, I won't. I'll keep moving forward, I'll keep giving others hope. For them... and for you.'

I choke up a little.

'I won't ever forget you... I don't want to.'

I slowly let go and look back up at her, this time, she's in tears.

'I know you won't... and I'm so thankful for that.' She wipes away her tears, 'go now, do what you need to do, I'll be with you every step of the way, always.'

We both stand up, no longer standing in a thick ooze, but a colourful and serene water. She pats me on the shoulders, giving me a warm smile.

As everything begins to fade away, I see that same orb in front of us glow brightly into a luminescent light. I smile, knowing that I can do it, knowing that it's okay that I made my mistake.

Knowing that she's with me.

I don't think I'll ever forget these gnawing feelings of mine… but at least I'll be able to face them head on, knowing that it isn't just me who has to bear this alone.

I look into her eyes again, not with the chains and shackles of defeat, or the suffocating sorrow that once filled my heart, but with the hope that was always within me.

'Thank you. For everything.'

JAIDYN KEW (he/him) is a writer with an open-mindedness to all kinds of storytelling in whatever medium or form it may be, and a fascination towards otters and cheese.

Cambodia, September

Kiloran Hiscock

I'm on a study tour in Cambodia, working with an NGO
that helps women and children who've experienced severe
trauma. It's hot and humid. I drip with sweat and pretend I
don't care about looking nice, but when I'm talking to people,
I will the perspiration to stay inside my pores. Then I remember
where we are and berate myself for my superficial priorities.
Media students are making documentaries here, and I'm one
of two writing students brought along to create a social media
campaign for the tour. But it's unclear what's expected of me,
so when I'm not helping out the other students, I sit with my
laptop open and try to look busy even though I'm actually just
checking my emails. I'm doing this when I get a message from
my housemate Paul, who's back home in Melbourne. It seems
benign: he asks me if I've met up with Melanie yet – she's our
friend who lives in Siem Reap. I reply that I haven't, then I wait.
Seen: 3:30 pm. He doesn't respond.

A knot starts to form in my stomach. Why did he ask
me that? I tell myself it's a normal question, that I'm being
ridiculous. This feeling is familiar; it doesn't take much more
than having the phone ring for me to presume something
terrible has happened. Boyfriend goes off the radar in Spain?
He's lost in the wilderness with no water. Mother doesn't answer
her phone? She's probably been murdered. My rational mind
tells me it's improbable, but panic lives inside me, always.

I check my email. There's a new one from my other housemate, Sally, with no subject: *Can you call me at all? When yr able to x*

The knot in my stomach is more like a pit of snakes now. Something is wrong. My fingers start to shake, and it feels like I'm being hoisted into the sky like I'm bungee jumping in reverse. I realise I've been pacing the yard for about twenty minutes now, dialling my boyfriend's number several times, but he won't answer. Something has happened to him. I'm sure of it. Kat, a fellow student, walks past me and stops. 'Are you okay?' She looks concerned. I explain what's going on and she urges me to call Sally.

'I can't,' I say.

'You have to.'

'I'm scared I'll vomit.'

'Well if you do, that's okay.'

'But I don't want to call her because once I know... I can never go back.'

Kat is silent for a moment, then says, 'Well... there's that. But knowing is better than wondering. And you don't have control over whatever's happened. And shit happens – that's life.'

Her frankness touches me, so I sit down and call Sally. She answers with a muffled 'Hello?'

'Hi Sally.'

'Have you spoken to anyone yet?' She sounds dazed, robotic. I hear people in the background.

'No.'

'—passed away.' Her voice is muffled.

'I didn't hear you. Can you say that again?'

'Isabelle passed away.' And with those words, I get a sickening feeling I've only felt once before: a flood of relief that it wasn't someone else, competing with the utter horror of the truth – a horrible, inhuman cocktail of shock, shame and gratitude.

'What happened?'

She tells me, and it begins: the tears that leave my face red and irritated and swollen and flaky; that interrupt dinner; that alienate me from the teachers but compel the students to hug me, look me softly in the eyes, bring me food and care for me. The crying will break but won't ever really cease, because no tears will be enough to fill the void of death, and every time you lose someone else, you not only cry for them but for everyone before them too, and for yourself and what else you could lose. And that's the way it should be.

✕✕✕

I dreamt of her the other night. We're standing inside my shower, fully clothed, no water running. It must have been a misunderstanding because she is here. She is enveloping me with her arms and I can smell her sweet scent. Dead people can't hug, so it was all a misunderstanding. I look up at her, shiny black hair, eyes fixed forward, determination in her gaze. 'I'm going to get better,' she says.

My lungs fill with air as I breathe in fast. I'm too scared to speak but I collect the words from somewhere inside of me and ease them out of my lips, barely audible. 'Really? Are you sure?'

She holds me, her embrace unwavering, steady and present. 'I'm sure,' she says. '9.5 out of 10, I'm sure.'

KILORAN HISCOCK (she/her) is an actor, a freelance writer and an editor. She's written for a variety of print and online publications, including *Record Culture Magazine*.

What You Make Us, What We Make You

Cormac Mills Ritchard

Oh what horrors mirrors hold
when monsters behold them
who with one hand admonish means
the other hand had sold them,
while seeing not what joy and cheer
we share with one another
for such beauties aren't for those
who only would them smother.

Oh what horrors mirrors hold
where they have gilded frames
and those who on them smiling gaze
will never say our names,
the names they've bled and stamped
in mud as though us paving stones
will always break their fatal fall
and never break their bones.

Oh what horrors mirrors hide
for those who look them into.
For men of ivory spires will
never know what we have been through
to lay their empires brick by brick
and towers, stone by stone,
and think we'll never climb their stair
and throw them from their throne.

Oh what horrors mirrors hold
for those who can't afford them
and those for whom they shovel sand
choose never to reward them.
Yes, those who feed off paupers' plates
are praised for their invention,
and souls who fed their 'genius'
don't ever rate a mention.

Oh what horrors mirrors hold
where they have gilded frames
and those who on them smiling gaze
don't even know our names.
The bodies they have trampled on
show that their road to hell
is paved not with good intention
but shrapnel and bomb shell.

Oh what horrors mirrors hold
when monsters behold us
and seeing now what you have wrought
seek ever to forhold us.
But we have all the wit and strength
which greed from you grew:
as, yes, we built your castles but
we built your cannon too.

CORMAC MILLS RITCHARD (he/him) is a leading member of
Uni Students for Climate Justice who's helped organise some of the
largest climate rallies in Melbourne in recent years. He's a regular
environmental writer for *Red Flag* and a member of the RMIT
Socialist Alternative Club.

An Orangutan Called Harta

Heather Gallagher

This is an excerpt from a middle-grade novel,
My Brother the Orangutan.

M y Sherlock senses were on red alert.
Granny and Rex were loitering in front of the gold
elephant statue, debating which animal to see next. I moved
away; no need for people to know we were related. I pulled my
little black book from my backpack. On a fresh page, I wrote:

> Melbourne Zoo, 4:16 pm
>
> Present: Esther Powers (eleven and three quarters), Rex
> Powers (will be eight in two days) and Dot 'Granny'
> Powers (ancient).
>
> Potential crime: Wildlife smuggling?
>
> Suspects: Frazzled mother, running, with twins in
> stroller (always expect the unexpected); zoo attendant
> directing people into a cafe (strange! undercover
> baddie?); teacher herding pack of children (hmm)

'Esther dear!' Granny bumped my leg with her motor scooter.
Her face matched her beloved Red Baron. 'I'm so excited
about living with you all, I'd do cartwheels if I could,' she said.

'It's like I always say, family is the whipped cream that holds the lasagne of life together.'

Er, yes. Granny was the only good thing about moving to the city, but *that* was too painful to think about because *that* was the Second Worst Thing that had ever happened to me.

'Don't you mean white sauce, Granny?' I asked.

'Nope, whipped cream. It gives that extra creamy fluffiness.'

Ah, Granny. Her *MasterChef* obsession meant she was always cooking something or thinking about cooking something. Something dee-sgusting!

'Rexie wants to see the orangutans,' Granny said.

'That's nice.' I turned in the direction of the seals. The underground viewing area was the perfect place for a criminal mastermind. Also, it would be cooler. My 'Save the Bees' T-shirt was already sticking to me.

'Essie!' Rex grabbed my elbow.

'*Reichenbach*, Rex!' I yanked my arm free. I was *not* starting my new city life caving to Rex's demands.

'*Reichenbach*?' Granny asked.

'It's Esther swearing, Granny,' explained Rex. 'Some weird Sherlock-thing.' He pulled on the handle of the Red Baron, forcing Granny to change direction. 'We're going this way!' They zoomed back the way we'd come, looking for the turn-off to the orangutans.

Granny was supposed to be in charge, but she was letting Rex lead her through the exit-only path. A short cut to the orangutans. 'That's not the right way!' I yelled, running to catch up.

Inside the bamboo tunnel, I found Granny and Rex frozen, as if posing for a weird photo. 'What are you guys—'

An orangutan was meandering along the path towards us.

'Cool!' breathed Rex.

The orangutan stared at Rex. It bared its teeth.

A zookeeper appeared at a bend in the path. 'Don't make any sudden movements.' The orangutan stole a peek at her over its shoulder. 'Didn't you hear the announcement?' the keeper called accusingly. 'You're supposed to be sheltering indoors!'

Out the corner of my eye I saw other keepers, sneaking through the bamboo like stealthy soldiers. One perched opposite us with a tranquiliser gun.

The keeper crept closer. 'Just step calmly away.'

'Granny!' I tugged her arm. 'We need to *move*!' Granny began reversing the Red Baron like a drunk dodgem car driver. I scurried alongside her.

The zoo forecourt was empty when we stumbled back in. Granny manoeuvred the Red Baron behind a giant palm tree. I huddled alongside her, catching my breath, and peered out.

'Rex?' He was supposed to be right behind me.

He wasn't.

'Wait here, Granny.'

Back in the green corridor that led to the orangutans, I wove through the bamboo. It didn't take long to find Rex. He'd crouched as the ape moved towards him. It seemed magnetised by Rex's carrot top, reaching out a leathery hand to stroke his hair.

Rex slowly lifted his head, revealing an idiotic grin. He held out his hand, like you'd do for a strange dog to sniff. The orangutan bared its teeth again and gave Rex a high-five! My brother's face lit up like a year's worth of pocket money had fallen into his hands.

Meanwhile, the keeper peeled a banana. The orangutan eyed her. You didn't need to be a genius to see what it was thinking – fruit or freedom?

'Harta,' she called. 'Want a narney?'

Harta looked at Rex. Then he looked at the banana.

'That's it, Harta,' said the keeper. Her voice was low and singsong like one of the meditation podcasts we endure at home. 'There's a good boy.'

Harta gave Rex a glance and then loped towards the keeper. When he reached her, he grabbed the banana and stuffed it in his mouth. The keeper held out a hand, which the orangutan took. They wandered off towards the orangutan enclosure.

Rex sprung back to life. 'Did you see that?' he yelped. 'That was the coolest thing *ever*!'

It was cool, but I wasn't going to agree with him. 'You see, but you do not observe.' It was one of my top five Sherlock quotes.

'Huh?'

'Since when do animals at the zoo escape? It's a mystery!'

'Mystery?' croaked Gran.

I jumped. Gran had a way of appearing out of nowhere. 'Yes,' I told her. 'The mystery is – *how did he get out?*'

Illustrator: Odi Evans

HEATHER GALLAGHER (she/her) is a published children's author, book reviewer and award-winning journalist. She's passionate about children's literacy and works as a writer-in-residence in primary schools for the educational charity, Ardoch. Her latest picture book, *Scaredy Cat*, is based on her anxious dog, Pip. Please visit heathergallagher.com.au for more information.

End of a Friendship

Chloe Bloom

I am eight-years-old and the January sun is blistering my skin. As I tiptoe over sizzling concrete, the kiosk sign looms in the shade and a few gold coins press into my palm. The girl at the counter passes me a Paddle Pop Icy Twist packed in flimsy blue plastic and a killer python lolly in a white paper bag. My wet, chlorine-covered fingers leak through the paper as the sugary ice melts down my chin. When I reach the patch of grass lined by faded beach towels, the soles of my feet are red raw. I flop onto my stomach and watch ants trail along the brickwork that separates the dirt from the cement. My mum lathers my pink cheeks in another layer of 30+ sunscreen and I squirm, squinting at the sun.

There is another girl my age at the pool; her skin is peach-coloured by the sun and her long brown hair sticks to the back of her purple polka dot tankini. The girl is crying. There is a lick of deep crimson dripping down her knee. A woman scoops her up and brings her to a pile of beach bags under the shade of an umbrella. Her mum reminds me of mine. The mother's wide-rimmed sunglasses cover half her face. The tip of her nose is covered in green zinc.

There is another woman under the umbrella. She is wearing hibiscus-printed board shorts, similar to the sort my dad wears. She wipes the girl's knee clean with the edge of a towel and covers it with a bandaid and a kiss. She kisses the woman too. Although her lips do not seem to be bleeding.

⋊⋌⋊⋌

Taylor's newsfeed flickers.

She clenches my hand under the table. Her jagged nails dig into my palm. She has been biting them nervously all week. I sort of like the way it feels, but I would never say it out loud. It reminds me of when we were younger; two strange kids at the pool playing mermaids, opening our eyes underwater so we could find each other, chlorine turning our eyes bloodshot. Now that we are almost fifteen, she does not reach for me anymore. Not since everyone found out she has two mums.

Girls in our homeroom say it makes her weird. I do not see what is so weird about Taylor. Or her mums. Or the fact that she was the first girl in our grade to wear pants instead of a skirt. Or that her hair is short enough that she does not have to tie it up at school like everyone else.

She refreshes the website on her laptop screen for the seventh time. Out the window, thick grey clouds hang over the city. I can see the Skydeck, like a needle piercing the horizon. Not far from there is a sea of people drenched in rainbow outside Parliament House – Taylor's parents included.

'I feel sick,' Taylor whispers. 'They really want a summer wedding.'

I squeeze her hand. I do not know how to say it; to explain that I think I am like them too.

⋊⋌⋊⋌

The pub glows behind us as we stumble down the hill, bodies catching the moonlight as they hang along its vicinity. We left everyone quietly, but a part of me wants them all to see. I want a witness as she leads my sweaty hand in hers towards the beach. The night is an entanglement of slipped in kisses and boxed wine. I am afraid of what will happen when the sun comes up tomorrow.

We leave our shoes on the boardwalk and lead each other to the smoother sand that has been run over by the tide. We write our names with our feet and watch as the water dissolves our work. Waves crash and spray salt water on our bare legs. Taylor chases me along the shoreline until we collapse, limbs intertwined. Each kiss is annihilating. I imagine each one happening in a different place. The sand beneath my back transforms to the hard wood of my bedroom floor. The sky turns into a cinema screen. The ocean and the sound of its transient waves pulling in and out becomes the familiar drawl of a city bound train sprinting along its tracks.

'I love you,' I mumble through heavy, panting breaths.

Taylor's schoolies pass hangs from her neck, grazing my cheek as she pulls away.

'You know we can't do this Nat,' she says.

I cannot see her eyes in the dark. I hope this means she cannot see mine.

>×<×<×<

The way she tilts her eyes towards the table tells me I am already a stranger.

Suddenly I am small again, with burnt skin and a soggy killer python in my hand. She is the same at twenty-one as she was back then. Her dark hair is longer than it has ever been. She sits tall in her seat. This time she does not accept the chewy, artificial olive branch.

I am crying in a food court in the middle of the city, and the banh mi place has been playing nothing but Adele for the last twenty minutes. I feel overexposed, like a camera flash blinding me as I look into the lens and force a smile through my teeth.

I do not know what happened to us. My heart is open and empty; a Tupperware container lodged in the back of the pantry, stained by years of use and deep-red pasta sauce that will never come out.

Taylor remains still. I stare at the postcard I bought with her at the NGV an hour before. It is a black and white photograph of four women, hands linked and mouths gaping joyfully in front of a graffitied brick wall somewhere in Fitzroy. *'Lesbians are lovely!'* it reads. Her parents have the same print hanging in their dining room. I ache. I will never sit at their table again.

CHLOE BLOOM (they/she) is a writer, editor and bookseller living in Naarm. Their writing usually revolves around queerness and coming of age, sometimes bending into the horror genre. One day they will *maybe* finish their novel. Find them @finalgirlapologist (Instagram).

Central Park

Jennifer Matthews

There's nothing Edwardian civic fathers liked better than a park. So, in 1906, when the opportunity to buy 19 acres of land on the outskirts of suburbia cropped up, the Malvern Council seized it and created one. They laid it out with gardens to the south and an oval to the north, and though it was central to nothing at the time, they named it Central Park. As suburbia expanded, it grew into its name, and over a hundred years later, it is indeed at the centre of its community.

On a mild, blue day, I walk into the park from its quiet south-western corner. Elms shade its gravel paths. Rainbows of flowers circle its trees and rim its vivid green lawns. A sunburst of red geraniums matches a picnic rug on which lovers embrace. Hundreds of bridal parties have posed here for photos, and echoes of their laughter rustle through a bouquet of palm trees.

Along the path, fitness stations offer opportunities to do push ups. They culminate in a pod of sophisticated gym machines near the oval, where personal trainers cheer on their sweating clients.

In contrast to this hearty athleticism, the Malvern Tramways Band used to play here on Sunday afternoons. A kiosk with refreshments was erected in 1911. A supper room added in the 1920s was popular for dances and receptions. All are long gone.

Now, people sip their lattes at the cafes across Burke Road, near the corner where the tram clanks up Wattletree Road to the terminus. They gossip at pavement tables or take their coffee to park benches round the oval where, instead of music, they hear the hum of traffic and the cooing of crested pigeons. Like the cafes and traffic, crested pigeons were nowhere to be seen when the park was created. Climate change has driven them south.

The oval is the beating heart of Central Park. On bygone Sundays, public school boys and girls paraded around it to the music of the band, hoping to pick up. Today's teenagers hang out in heterogeneous groups chatting in the current teenage jargon. 'Like, I'm like "no way" and he's like, "whatever",' I hear them say.

Elderly couples stroll by arm in arm. Kindergarten kids whiz around on training bikes. Walkers stride past, bum bags strapped around their waists, water bottles in hand, physiological measuring devices strapped to their arms.

Serious runners also pound around the oval. It is named after local John Landy, world record holder, Olympic bronze medallist and Governor of Victoria. Today's runners keep up the good work, T-shirts soaked with sweat, muscles pumping, breath rasping.

It is in the centre of the oval that the main drama unfolds. Here festivals, concerts and primary school sports days are held, and the thwack of cricket balls can be heard every weekend in summer. But its greatest value is that it is a dog-off-leash area.

Large dogs and small, thoroughbreds and bitzers tumble about, sniff each other's bottoms and compete to fetch balls. Their owners, wielding ball-throwing implements, stretch and chat.

I sit under a magnificent red gum and watch, inhaling the smell of freshly mown grass. Like most other gums in the park, this tree is not native to the area. No trees survive from the days when the Bunurong people had it to themselves.

A row of kurrajongs is all that remains of an avenue in honour of slain soldiers. The avenue is forgotten, but the fallen are not. Flowers ceremonially cover the war memorial on the corner every Anzac Day.

Clouds gather as I walk back through the gardens, passing a playground – all squeals and slides – a wedding-cake fountain and a heritage-listed conservatory. On the corner, where the paths through the park diverge, two girls fly into each other's arms, ponytails swishing. The sun breaks out again.

This is where I started. I have come full circle.

JENNIFER MATTHEWS (she/her) is a Melbourne-based freelance writer of fiction and non-fiction. She's currently working on a crime novel.

15%

Callan Walsh

Sabres of honey sunlight puncture the gumleaf canopy, speckling the rocks with gold glowing coins. Foreign rubber footfall stamps them out. In fawn treated leather, blunted by exhaustion, the chugging steps of a hiker lone and quiet on the trail.

With a half hour yet to crest the mountain, she rests a moment in the cups of a cavernous outcrop carved by eons of wind into the undulant form of flicked silk. She drinks until her breath snags in her neck and drips roll from her lip. Her chest is clear and lighter here, her head cloudless.

As the sun begins to tint orange as waning lamplight, she digs her pockets for her hourly cursory glance at her phone.

4:29 pm	SOS only	15% 🔋

Battery saver mode on

Unknown number
Is that really you in the pics?

Her brow creases, carving tiny couloirs for her beading sweat. She regards the sun casting dimly down the claws of the craggy ranges. With her forefingers, she tightens her shoelace, her back knuckles knotted white on the corner of her thick phone case. Appraising the hour, she pursues the crest of the mountain, setting broad striding boot prints in the soft sun-speckled soil of the trail.

Slowly languishing light bends along the path, gilding twig and grass alike, and the phone in her hand vibrates twice.

4:54 pm		11%

Battery saver mode on

Unknown number
You're beautiful. I want to take you up on that offer.

Edwin
hi babe how's the hike going?
when will you be coming home?
do u still want to head off before dark?
babe? i can see you reading these messages

Me
Hey babe, I'm so close to the top! Maybe a bit after dark? I'm not getting another chance to do this hike, so I have to make it all the way! Service is really patchy here so I couldn't see any messages until now? Also I'm still getting those weird scam texts

Edwin
weird
hey so i just saw your new post
wtf??
can we at least talk about it?

Me
What post?

Your message could not be sent
SOS only

From a nearer vantage, the crest swells into a bloated belly of bushland, cradling chittering fledglings and sprinkled insects among the mustered dusk-lit gums. She slumps against a trunk and gulps her drink again. Revealed through the interstices of the canopy, in the penumbra of the mountain's ridge, the latticed red skeleton of a telecommunications tower.

5:11 pm   ıll   8% ▭

Battery saver mode on

Unknown number
Hey girl wats good im a big man gonna wreck u 9 inches
image

Unknown number
I'm waiting outside you're house Grey Toyota camry
image

Edwin
the instagram one wtf
i know you have service, I can see you reading my messages
call me please

The sun pitches purplish into the cliffs as she sits nibbling the nails of her twitching fingers, breathing with quivering chills beneath the chirping branches. Her sinewed neck pulses red. Her thumb tip clicks gingerly against the glass.

~~Ive decided Im going to make some changes in my life. Ive realised that I am a very sensual person. I feel Im very in touch with my erotic self. Being with my boyfriend is not enough for me and we have talked and made an agreement about what we are doing moving forward and I am feeling very liberated and ready to explore! Hmu for fun times ;)~~

Post deleted

Me
Wtf my account's been hacked. That picture
is from my camera roll like a week ago. I'm
actually freaking out this is fucking weird
How long has it been up?

Edwin
are you serious?

Me
Wtf I'm not joking!
I've gotta change my passwords now
gimme a sec

Unknown number
Your so hot in those pictures

Unknown number
U like to be tied up and gagged?

The red sun flares against the rim of the earth, trimming the tracks of her tears with brilliant ruby, like lacquer dripping over her horripilated skin. Leaves rush tight together and flowers bend in the wind, bound fast to the ground by feeble stem.

5:21 pm   5%
Battery saver mode on

Edwin
Mil your facebook, all our photos
you gotta delete your account or something fuck
they posted the video from the hotel
i'm calling the police this is fucked

Your Facebook account has been deleted

Shadows stretch bold and black over every living thing, flooding the mountain in massive muting darkness. Birds huddle sedate and silent in the trees, and the bushland freezes soundless but for leaves rattled by a dull, gelid breeze.

The cloak of night covers the woman, her face lit sickly pale by the screen and collared by thin stabs of vapour breath like the gnarled knuckles of ghouls tightening around her neck.

5:34 pm   ı|ı   2% ▭

Battery saver mode on

Tom

I know we havent talked in a while. Two years exactly. I still think about you all the time. I still miss you sometimes. I used to wonder what I did wrong. All the things I couldve done different. But now I know none of it was my fault. Id do anything for you but youre just too selfish to care.
It's funny that this is the first time youve changed your password since I met you.
Delete all the accounts you want. You cant delete this
pornhub.com/user/camillapirainoisawful

Camilla Piraino's Porn Videos.

About Camilla: Im a 26yo with hot body and ugly personality! I have a fantasy of strange men coming to my house looking for sex, any time day or night, my address is [address] and my phone number is [number] so please do your worst! Check my pics and videos below ;)

Me

It's Tom my ex tell the cops h

Battery depleted
Shutting down

In the black, in the cold bristled bush, she sets her head on its side against the dirt. All the animals are nestled quiet and invisible in branches and burrows, and the flowers have all closed. Camilla, too, stills herself – deaf and blind and cradled in the mute, empty earth.

CALLAN WALSH (he/him) works in creative and technical writing, often drawing from both disciplines to inform his varied stylistic approach. He has been published in Tone Deaf, *Visible Ink Anthology*, and multiple zines and guerrilla publications. Read more of his work at callanwalsh.com, @callan.ambulance (Instagram and Threads) and @calwzw (Twitter/X).

The Morning After

Claudia Lyons

This is an excerpt from a larger work,
Thank You for Your Patience.

Gregory awoke from a fitful sleep. Grey light peeked through the gaps in the curtain, casting ethereal shadows on the far wall. The small of his lower back ached and the joint of his right knee flamed. A sack of rocks would be more comfortable than this damned mattress, he thought, reaching for the blister pack on his bedside table. He felt the cool foil brush his fingertips before the packet toppled to the floor.

'Oh, for Christ's sake!' It sounded feeble, even to his own ears. Grumbling, he pushed at the duvet and dragged his legs from its suffocating weight. The floorboards were like ice. Margaret had always been on him about getting a rug for the bedroom. Gregory was relieved to feel his slippers where he'd left them; he slipped his feet into their sheepskin comfort. With great care, he manoeuvred his body upright and braced a hand on the wall so that he could peer at the floor. The pills had probably tumbled into the abyss beneath his bed – the bastards. He considered getting down on his hands and knees to look. Really, the humiliation if he couldn't get back up… What would he do? Call for a neighbour? Call triple zero?

You have dialled emergency triple zero.
Your call is being connected.

The memory slammed into his chest. The bank girl. Her scream. He'd called Fiona, then dialled triple zero.

Do you need police, fire, or ambulance?

Gregory's arm buckled, causing his shoulder to smack into the wall. Pain reverberated all the way to his teeth. Wisps of the previous night muddled in his brain.

'Get a grip on yourself,' he muttered. There would be more pills in the pantry. All he really needed was a good strong cuppa.

A chill in the kitchen gave form to Gregory's breaths so that they hung like ghosts before him. His walking cardigan was draped over a dining chair; he wrapped it tight around himself, being careful not to jostle his shoulder. Pursing his lips, he snuck a look towards the bedroom before reaching for the control unit fixed to the wall. He pressed the circular, red button that he'd learnt meant 'on'. A faint hum began as the central heating kicked in. Old age had clearly softened him – how Margaret would crow if she knew.

Amelia.

That'd been her name – the girl at the bank. Or maybe it was the triple zero operator? No, he was sure it must've been the name of the bank girl. Gregory stared at the wall. Amelia. His heart clenched. Blinking hard, he turned and picked up the kettle, then carried it to the sink to fill. The triple zero operator hadn't seemed particularly concerned. Her voice had been smooth and as toneless as the automated recording that'd greeted him. He couldn't be sure that he'd spoken to a person at all in the end. Surely it wouldn't be legal to have emergency services totally dependent on robots, although the government *were* capable of all manner of idiocy. They'd made that clear when they put machines in charge of the supermarket check-outs.

Cold water splashed over his hand, forcing his attention to the overflowing kettle. Bugger. Gregory slopped the excess water over the side and then placed the kettle on its base. The central heating was purring, and he could feel it already warming his bones. It seemed to soothe some of his angrier aches. Marvellous invention. Still no match for a good roaring fire, of course, but decent all the same.

Gregory reached into the overhead cupboard for a mug, then paused. His favourite – no-nonsense, burgundy, with a sensible *G.H* printed in gold serif font – was absent. It must've been in the dishwasher. Instead, his hand remained hovering over a mug that'd caught his eye. Fiona had given it to Margaret some Mother's Day morning decades ago. He couldn't remember the year exactly – they all blurred together at a certain point. But the mug was still here. It was a tacky piece of crap, really – a garish shade of pink, featuring a pop-eyed pug bearing a wide grin beneath the slogan *PUG LIFE.*

Margaret had shrugged when he'd poked fun. 'I like its silliness,' she'd say.

Gregory dropped a teabag into the offensive mug and poured the steaming water in. After fetching a crisp blister pack from the pantry (the central heating was good but not *that* good), he carried the mug carefully to the living room and placed it down on a floral coaster atop the side table. His armchair faced the window, where the street could be viewed through sun-bleached lace curtains. Outside, the yard was steeped in wan light. The rose bushes that'd been Margaret's pride were bare and gnarled, posted like sentries along the low brick fence. He'd yet to fix the sprinklers, and the grass had withered to spite him. A few weeds poked impishly from the garden beds. Frost was already melting from their misshapen leaves. It couldn't be long past dawn.

Gregory tugged a bright, crocheted rug over his knees. There were few comforts more precious than a throw across the lap while settled in one's favourite chair. Yesterday's newspaper sat folded on the side table, open to the cryptic crossword that he hadn't yet finished. The clue for 9-down was proving to be a real stumper – a bloody Broadway play of all things. That was really more in Margaret's wheelhouse.

He stared blankly at the empty armchair to his right. Between the two of them, they'd practically set records. Now it seemed he could barely finish one.

CLAUDIA LYONS (she/her) is a freelance writer and editor with a passion for storytelling. While she adores crime thrillers, Claudia also loves reading across genres and savouring literary fiction. She works as a banker, and as a blog writer for the digital-marketing group Envato.

Hope Springs Eternal

Jake Egan

My name is... actually, no. You don't need to know my name. My father was obsessed with our family name and living up to the expectations that went along with it. 'Why aren't you willing to give what it takes?' he'd always ask me. I'm so much more than a name. I'm a woman. I'm a creator of life. I can feel the life inside me right now, kicking and pushing at my stomach. I'm sitting on a creaky old chair in an empty house. I'm alone, but I'm never alone anymore. She's with me. I've already given her a name; Hope. My Hope.

Lightning flashes brightly outside, illuminating the room with blue light like the burst of a moon-sized camera. A second later, thunder cracks so loud I lift my hands to cover my ears. Hope kicks excitedly inside my womb; she makes me smile. She'll be a dancer, I'm certain of it. As the rain begins to smash down on the tin roof, my waters break. I force myself to breathe through the initial panic. 'I can do this,' I tell myself. My bag is already packed and by the door. I grab the keys, walk out to the car and drive through the relentless rain to hospital. To my Hope.

The hospital room is filled with beige space-age looking instruments like hospital rooms the world over. A curtain divides me from another pregnant woman, waiting in purgatory. She's older, and her husband slouches uncomfortably in a plastic seat next to her bed. She gave me that look as I came into the room. It doesn't bother me anymore. It's a look I've become used to as a soon-to-be teenage mum.

The woman and her husband are silent, drifting in and out of sleep. The night outside is pitch black, apart from the intermittent flashes of lightning. The rain hasn't stopped. The smell of bleach and cleaning products is overpowering. I'm restless; I know my Hope isn't far away. I can't wait to meet her.

My midwife's name is Maryam. She's fit and about five feet tall. I see her knowing and resourceful eyes behind her hijab. She looks young, and I ask if we're the same age. She laughs kindly and tells me she's in her thirties with eight children of her own. Seven boys and her youngest is a girl. She gave birth to her daughter alone, in the bathroom at home, while her husband was at work and her boys were at school. I wonder what car they own. It would have to have a minibus, at least. Maryam tells me I'm doing a great job. She tells me I'm strong for doing this on my own. She promises to be with me for the entire journey. 'Hope will be perfect and magical,' she assures me. Maryam is the first person I've shared Hope's name with.

When the pain intensifies, it's like nothing I've felt before. It's pure agony. The contractions feel as if someone's trying to wring out my insides like a wet towel. But part of me relishes the feeling because it means I'm totally present. I'm here, in this body, in this hospital, in extreme pain. I have a nagging sense that something's wrong, but I shush that voice inside of me. This is what's supposed to happen. I've seen enough movies to know that the woman shrieks in pain. Then the baby arrives screaming and bright red. The mother holds the little body against her chest, crying and laughing with joy. 'This is what one must go through to become a mother,' my mum would say if she were here. I wonder what my dad would say. Would he finally see I could do what it takes for things that actually matter?

Maryam is true to her word; she's with me the entire time. Through the thick clouds of pain, I notice her calm and confident demeanour change to concern. There are always machines beeping in hospitals, so I don't notice at first. But the beeps grow louder and become alarms. Lights are flashing and suddenly there's lots of people and voices surrounding me. They talk quickly and use words I don't understand. The doctors feel inside of me, to my Hope. The lightning outside finds its way inside me, it's my pain. Electricity shoots through me over and over. All I see are flashes of light followed by darkness. 'Stay with me and keep pushing,' Maryam's voice is confident and encouraging as she squeezes my hand. It feels sweaty, like she's been holding it for hours.

Everything changes then. The world has inverted.

⋈⋈⋈

In the seconds we were together, I shared everything with my Hope. A lifetime of love condensed into a moment. She was everything I dreamed of.

Birth. Death. Hope.

I didn't want to die, but in that moment, I was willing to give my life. I knew, I'd been put on this Earth for her.

Live on, my Hope. Keep dancing. I'll be watching.

JAKE EGAN (he/him) is a novel writer and screenwriter. He writes in various genres but leans into sci-fi and fantasy. He worked with *The New York Times* best-selling author Alison Goodman on his last manuscript, *Shadow & Snow*. When not writing, he's running, reading or sleeping.

Scars

Katy Hocking

My piece-of-shit laptop dies again. The night I was admitted, Max tried to hang himself with a laptop charger and ever since they've been more regulated than crack. I know this for a fact because the greasy guy two rooms down offered me some last night.

I slam my laptop closed. Would it really be much of a loss if I threw it out the window?

'I'm sorry, Indi,' he whispers. Max is a quiet guy, his shoulders hunched, his sad eyes never meeting yours. I think he lives most of his life inside his head – dangerous for people like us.

'Hey.' I smile, reaching across the wobbly dining table and patting his hand. The dining area is mostly empty this late at night, but I lower my voice just in case. 'Who among us hasn't at least thought of doing it? I think the laptop charger idea was kind of clever.'

His lips twitch – that's as good as a beaming smile for him – and I feel proud. I've heard people call him creepy, but I find him interesting.

'That's what I was aiming for. Clever. I thought about slitting my wrists, but it seemed too messy.' He pauses, his lips twitching again. 'Not to mention clichéd.'

My smile slips. I force a bark of laughter through numb lips. His eyes meet mine for a second then dart back to the ground.

✕✕✕

Indi's gone. She's *gone*. I search the whole ward and still can't find her. Black spots appear in my vision, and I have to stop and take some deep breaths.

I hate this. It's easier to not care.

I ask a nurse. The cranky one. She huffs and pinches the bridge of her beaky nose. 'Her mum has taken her out for the day. Now, shoo, Max.'

I pace the ward, gnawing on the inside of my cheek until I taste blood. She signs back in a little after noon. I wave, but she doesn't notice. Her eyes are glazed and puffy, her face pale with blotchy red patches. She moves mechanically, stiff. I watch her until her door clicks shut. I want to offer comfort.

I don't know how.

✕✕✕

Max's lips twitch as he pulls out a joint from his cigarette packet. It's still dark. The weeds growing between the cracks in the concrete are dusted with frost, the crappy outdoor furniture wet with dew.

He lights the joint then hands it to me. 'I thought you might need some cheering up.'

'What? Oh no, I'm okay.'

I take a hit anyway, the taste of the smoke comforting and familiar. He knows I'm lying, but he doesn't push. I like that about him. I take another hit, waiting for the floaty feeling, then pass it back. Puff, puff, pass and all that.

He shifts from foot to foot, his mouth opening and closing like he wants to say something, then decides not to.

'You'd make a good goldfish,' I say, throwing him a smirk.

His brows scrunch together. 'Huh?'

'Just say whatever it is you want to say.'

He pauses, eyes settling on a spot above my shoulder. 'Why are you here?'

'Well, currently I'm enjoying a joint with a friend.' I watch the smoke as it wriggles from the joint in his fingers, disappearing into the morning fog.

'You know that's not what I meant. You're different from the rest of us in here, less – for lack of a better word, *crazy*. You seem, I dunno, not happy, but not a complete mess either.'

My smile drops, all of the joy squeezes out of me like a dirty dish sponge, and I tug on the sleeve of my shirt. 'You should know by now not to judge someone by how they *seem.'*

My tone makes something in him retreat. His already hunched shoulders curve inwards, like he hopes he can fold in on himself and disappear. His gaze drops to his feet again. I didn't notice until that moment how open he has become with me. To watch it disappear like the smoke makes my heart hurt.

'You're right. I'm sorry.' He drops the joint. He can't get away from me fast enough.

'No, Max, I'm sorry.' I grab his arm. 'You just picked at a poorly healed scab.' I push up the sleeve of my hoodie. They're still raw, only just transformed from wounds to scars. I run my finger along the biggest. Thick and angry-red. It starts at my wrist and traces the vein upwards. I close my eyes, unable to look at them any longer. They're ugly, disgusting even. I hold them out, a peace offering, letting them speak the words that I can't.

My heart pounds in my ears. I start to think maybe he's gone, maybe the scars disgust him too. I hear the scuffing of shoes on concrete, then fingers trace the scar softly, like a feather, giving me goosebumps. He pulls the sleeve down and takes my hand.

I squeeze. He squeezes back.

KATY HOCKING (she/her) is a writer from Melbourne, currently living in Wallan. She dreams of being a successful author and is working on an upper middle-grade fantasy novel. After graduating, Katy plans to do further study to become a librarian.

Bratwurst Delacroix and the Twelve Deaths of Christmas

Heath John Ramsay

This is an excerpt from a larger work,
Yours Truly, Ethan Blake.

Bratwurst Delacroix, who loathed his first name almost as much as he despised domesticated animals, was swirling a snifter of stolen brandy when he hatched a plan to kill a neighbour's pet on each of the twelve days of Christmas.

Sitting in a cobalt blue artisanal lawn chair the least kind of his neighbours referred to as 'the throne', he savoured the hot sting of brandy as he swished it through his teeth, appreciating its ability to sterilise his mouth as it dispersed his thoughts.

> Mandy is whipped by that stupid dog of hers... Pudding is a sometimes food... Jasmine's husband can barely conceal his *fabulous* secret... Imagine how joyous it would feel to kill Mandy's miniature poodle... Merry Christmas Mandy, Chutney's DEAD! ... Yes bitch! The time is now... Let's get lethal.

It was something about the way Mandy pandered to Chutney that led to the death-to-pets seed taking root – a grotesque display of accommodation that involved Mandy unravelling herself from a leash-tangle instigated by Chutney, while praising him for being a 'cheeky devil'. It was Chutney in the lead and Mandy – the ever-obliging tinsel-primped lemming – forever tethered to Chutney's shadow. Bratwurst wasn't having a bar of it.

> Mandy, you freak bitch, you let that yap-yap run you like a river... *how embarrassing*. Don't worry Mandy, I'll gladly steer you back to the natural order of things – one serving of popcorn poodle coming up!

As Bratwurst was a staunch devotee of catastrophic thought escalation, it was but a moment before the death-to-pets seed blossomed, multiplied and manifested as a neighbourhood-pet kill list which also served as a poetic reimagining of Bratwurst's most beloved Christmas carol – *The Twelve Days of Christmas*.

> Note to self: Draft death-to-pets manifesto pronto... That's one glorious foray into animal cruelty each day for twelve days... Merry Christmas, Bratwurst! You've outdone yourself yet again... Can I have an M for Maverick, please!

Bratwurst licked his lips, leaning forward to admire the most ordered and well-kept front porch on Cardinal Close – the debris-free patio a testament to his thrice-weekly sweeping regime. The only whimsey was a flourish of iridescent pink petunias cascading like a giant tongue over the boulder wall of his Serenity Alcove. Pink meant more to Bratwurst than just being his signature colour. Rose pink was the blush of his cheeks when he first realised his attraction to his former 'best friend' Scott. Hot pink was the colour of the chaise longue where Scott's father proved his curiosity was anything but idle. Twilight was lavender pink on the evening Scott went missing shortly after.

Paradise pink was the water surrounding Scott's corpse as his blood leeched through the shallows of his neighbour's koi pond. Champagne pink was the colour of death by 'accident'. Bright pink was the shade of bloodshot in Scott's father's eyes when he truly understood the meaning of '*two can keep a secret if one of them is dead.*'

> Pink for erotica... Pink for denial... Pink for feminine ferocity... Pink for survival.

As Bratwurst ruminated on such fond memories, it occurred to him that making an assortment of pet-sized patchwork blankets to gift his grieving neighbours served as both a delightful twist of the knife and a blessed red herring. No-one would assume that a patchwork blanket maker and gift giver was guilty of anything other than poor taste and poor timing. Little would they know it was he who had microwaved their miniature poodles, woodchipped their kittens and dry-roasted their canaries.

Bratwurst swivelled in his chair to accommodate the increasing pressure in his crotch and caught the evil grin spreading across his face in the emergency mirror he kept beneath the Strawberry Ice agapanthus beside his front door.

> Hello little canaries... I'm Bratwurst, and I'll be ushering you to the afterlife this afternoon... Jasmine is out playing golf with her friend who shouldn't wear pleats and will probably never think to look for you in her Weber BBQ... I'll start you on a low heat, just warm enough to ruffle your feathers... but then, my pretties, I'm going to turn the dial to full-blown scorch and record it on my iPhone to 'enjoy' later.

Bratwurst poured the last of the brandy he'd pinched from Mandy's pantry during the progressive dinner party the night before. He was confident she'd notice it was missing, and the thought that he'd served her an annoying and unsolvable domestic mystery enchanted him. The thing about the Mandys of the world – well, lemmings in general – was that they weren't worthy of the lives they so frivolously squandered. Items such as Remy Martin XO brandy were *wasted* on Blandy Mandy and her ilk – the other vapid residents of Cardinal Close. Bratwurst was delighted to find himself uninvited to dinner for the third year in a row and snuck a pantry wank *and* the brandy – a symbol of being far too extraordinary to be considered as a guest.

> Mandy, you fuck-chop, Christmas is an annual event, wouldn't you say? No, you wouldn't because you're a vacuous mess of a human with a disordered pantry full of products you've purchased because they were expensive and shiny, making you feel excited about something for the briefest of moments. Well guess what Mandy? Time's up. There are desert geckos more worthy of the oxygen you fritter away.

> Hmmm, kitten fritters...

><><

In the many years Phil Masters had been an English teacher, he'd been privy to all manner of grotesque, bawdy, anaemically underwritten and painfully overwritten creative writing attempts, but this was first time he'd felt deeply disturbed. Phil felt uneasy, then concerned and finally galvanised to act. Perhaps if he'd imbibed the fourth glass of cabernet merlot he'd cautioned himself against, he might have been jollier and the sense of menace he'd caught may not have landed so successfully. As it were though, it was caution that made a target of Phil Masters and overt caution that cost him the use of his vocal cords, forcing him into early retirement.

HEATH JOHN RAMSAY (he/him) is a sub-average singer, private dancer, pop culture glutton, former colourist at Elevation Hair & Beauty and enrolments advisor at the Phoenix Institute (raided by the Australian Federal Police in March 2016). He enjoys French knitting and *Murder, She Wrote*, and is currently reading *Balancing Act: the authorized biography of Angela Lansbury.*

Behind Closed Doors

Jarrod Sultana

This is an excerpt from a larger work.

It's the summer of 2004 and I'm eleven years old. 'This love' by Maroon 5 is topping the charts and the prime minister is John Howard.

My mates and I huddle behind the hill of our primary school back oval. We weren't allowed to be there, which only added to our excitement. On the way to school, we'd 'scabbed' one of the Target catalogues from someone's mailbox. We're turning the pages in anticipation, searching for the underwear section. I was just beginning to become sexually aware, but my mates were a year older.

We passed the catalogue around; our hands down our pants, laughing and commenting on the girl's bodies – everyone except me.

My attention was on the person next to the girl. I looked at the man and noticed how well he fitted into his tight briefs. I admired his tanned skin, large muscly arms and amazing six-pack.

That's when I knew I was different, even though I didn't understand it.

It was the first time I felt aroused, which was exciting but also scary because my mates noticed that it wasn't the girl who had given me a hard-on.

I lost my friends that day.

The rest of primary school was difficult for me. It was bad enough my surname was 'Sultana' – which was already fuel for certain kids to tease me – but I also became known as the 'faggot'.

I didn't know what that meant so I asked Mum and Dad one day. They responded with; 'something that isn't natural.'

I remember at a family gathering, my uncle once told me through drunken slurs, 'If you see any faggots on the street, make sure you beat them up, fuckin degenerates. Used to get 'em in high school in the seventies, fuckin smashed 'em after school, I did.'

Everyone in the room laughed.

><><

It's 2008, I'm fifteen years old and in high school. 'Use somebody' by Kings of Leon is playing on repeat through my MP3 player. The world is changing drastically, and Kevin Rudd is now prime minister.

I finally understood what being 'gay' meant, but I still didn't want to accept that I was.

I tried my best to hide it and convince myself and others around me. However, I couldn't fool the one person who became the best friend anyone could ask for!

Candice was a short Portuguese girl with freckles.

She'd transferred to our school from Geelong. She was 'pro-gay' which I'd never heard of before.

I still laugh when I think back to my 'coming out' to her.

'So, I've got something to tell you. . .' I said, voice shaky. 'But you can't tell anyone.'

She frowned and looked up at me from the maths homework we were doing. 'Um, hello, have you actually met me?'

'I think I like girls. . .' She raised an eyebrow. '—and boys.'

She let out one of her Candice squeals and forced me into a hug. 'Finally!'

'Wait, you knew?' I said, naively confused.

'No shit, babe, I've been waiting for you to tell me, like, forever. Oh my god, we can talk boys. They suck!'

It's still one of my fondest memories with her – and we've had many of them.

Still, no matter how much we talked, and to Candice's frustration, I continued to see that being gay was wrong.

Every time I had sex with a girl, I would try to convince myself that this was where I wanted and needed to be (which was just as unfair to them as it was to me and remains one of my deepest regrets).

I think the most brutal feeling a person can have is wanting and wishing to be someone else.

Just when I thought life couldn't get any more confusing, I had my first boy crush. His name was Connor. A Zac Efron look-a-like; a big flirt with a dangerous smile. Straight as they came and the popular, high school bad boy. He was always nice to me though and once we started attending more classes together, we formed a close friendship.

The best thing about having Connor as a friend (aside from his unearthly good looks and charm) was that he just didn't give a fuck about what people thought. It was exactly the kind of attitude I desperately needed in my life at the time.

At camp, I shared my first kiss with Connor – a meaningless and innocent game of spin-the-bottle to everyone else, but me. It was a defining moment I'll never forget. I no longer had any doubt or denial about my feelings.

After many long, sulky, pining conversations with Candice over the next six months, I decided to come clean and tell Connor everything.

'I think I like you,' I mumbled so fast I'm not even sure I knew what I'd just said.

He flashed that perfect smile of his. 'As in...'

I could feel myself going red in the face. 'Please don't make me say it again.'

'Come here, Jarrod.' He pulled me in and for a moment we stared into each other's eyes, not saying a word.

My heart was racing – this was my gay Cinderella moment... until it wasn't.

'You know I'm not gay, right? I love you; you know that – but as a friend. To be honest, I kind of like Candice.'

I spent many long nights crying into my pillow (and went through many ice-cream tubs).

The worst part was when Mum asked why I was so sad and I couldn't tell her. Or my sister. Definitely not my dad. Not even Candice. Not anyone.

JARROD SULTANA (he/him) enjoys reading young-adult fantasy fiction and is currently working on his debut novel of the same genre. His goal is to create and share relatable stories that capture and reflect the experiences of under-represented minority and marginalised people. Follow @JarrodSultana (Twitter/X).

Metamorphosis

Ethan Lewis-Granland

It began when I was young. A lingering resentment in my father's eyes, a disappointed sigh from my mother. With every passing judgment from them my body became more twisted.

The early days of the change had been the most painful. My bones weakened, then gnarled into grotesque shapes, and my hair slowly came loose from my scalp. The shadow I cast grew longer, stranger. With every avoided glance, every strike, every act of isolation, I felt it grow. So I crawled upstairs to my room and closed the door.

The room where I live is spotless. I make sure to clean the refuse and dust. If I ever left mess, my mother would punish me. I no longer leave mess.

I don't feel like getting out of bed today. The white drapes brush against my stomach, the frame of the window rattling in the breeze. The biting cold brings dread with it, and a heralding sun casts a harsh light over the room.

The bed sags under my frame, groaning with effort. Air passes through my lungs with difficulty as I try to haul myself up. Exasperated, I roll from one side to the other to build momentum.

With a loud thump I flip over the side and onto my stomach. The floorboards groan under my feet as I lift my amorphous self. The bare room embraces a cold science, every particle acting as though it were trying to eject me from its space.

The wood scrapes and scratches under my chitinous feet.

The railing holds fast as I crawl down the stairs, heaving myself to the ground floor.

I shuffle through the rooms to feel out the changes of the house. Each day it tilts and warps but whether this is from my own mind twisting or actual changes in the house, I'm never sure. The doorframes can barely contain my shell, but the rooms feel twice as large as yesterday.

My mother and father are already seated and eating in the kitchen. They keep their eyes down at their plates, the only sound passing between them being the clatter of metal on porcelain. My bowl has been filled with the same flavourless soup as always, and bread that has been stewing in it. It's a murky brown with pieces of cabbage floating around. It will sustain me for now.

I hear my father inhale a shaky breath as I enter, my thorax brushing his chair as I pass on twisted legs. My mother spares me a glance. I long for her to look at me in anything other than disgust. My body has grown large and fat. My arms and legs have shrunk, grown spikes and formed a strange crystalline shell.

I heave and slide towards my bowl. The soup is cold and lumpy as I swirl my claws to feel the texture. I scoop a small amount into my mouth and am surprised to taste a sugary flavour. My father could have poisoned it. It wouldn't be the first time he's tried. Perhaps this time it'll work.

They eat loudly behind me and talk about anything and everything else. I eat.

The soup doesn't do much to stave off my hunger. They never give me anything substantial to strengthen me, as I might change unexpectedly and escape. It's better to keep me weak and drained, feeding the shadow instead.

I look up at my father, sucking down the last bit of soaked bread. His eyes betray his awareness of me – dark rings and a twitch of the lower lid. Perhaps it's that he hasn't fully withdrawn me from his mind that keeps me from becoming altogether unrecognisable. He still hasn't let me go.

I look to my mother. She glows a touch more with each deepening shadow within me, her life returning. It's with pleasure that she feeds and keeps me. She stands to clear the table and her foot lands on my claw. My shell crunches beneath her weight and I chirp in pain. My decline returns her youth. She feasts on my despair.

I retreat to the main hallway. The front door remains locked with chains, a trickle of sunlight creeping through the cracks. I chitter. The promise of the outdoors, of freedom, seems a woeful impossibility. I have no plans, no future ahead. Just my shell and the slow tightening grip of isolation.

The weight of my body sags down to the ground. My parents continue to talk and clean behind me. I drag myself up and, with one last look at my parents, shuffle up to my room. With each scratchy step their voices grow louder, their laughs more boisterous. An emptiness closes in, choking me.

The isolation within the attic opens its arms and eagerly awaits me to fall into it once again. I embrace its comforting loneliness away from them.

Note: This work makes literary reference, and draws some parallels, to Franz Kafka's 1915 novella, *Metamorphosis*.

ETHAN LEWIS-GRANLAND (he/they) is a freelance copyeditor with a passion for spoken-word storytelling. He's worked previously at Writers Victoria and Oxford Publishing Press.

When I Am Alone

Brandon Simeoni

When I am alone, in the hours unknown to man, I change. One by one I slip into something that is softer on my joints and fits my frame. Does a soul, if it were real, have a shape?

The nature of the change means that I can only do it alone. Since it is a visceral experience, changing, I have to want to do it. I have tried forcing it but it makes me feel sick. Sicker than I usually feel, so I just wait for it to come. Waiting, for anyone as impatient as me, feels as though I am stuck in a sort of limbo. It is hell. Say I want to watch a film or go out to eat, or maybe go on a walk around the great park behind my house; I cannot. Because if I am in the middle of doing any of these things and the change yearns from within, I must cut the activity short to traipse back home and lock my bedroom door.

You can imagine how difficult it is to make friends. Especially since no-one knows that version of myself. When I am out for drinks, chatting, this feeling settles into the crevices of my skin like a weighted blanket, reminding me that none of these people can see what I see when I am alone. With that I will catch the first tram home. As it hums along the rails in the darkness of the city I struggle to hold my tears in. The notion that once I am home I can change, and all will be well in that pocket of solitary space-time keeps them at bay.

When I change, it feels as though my internal stars align causing a rush that floods the nerves along my skin. On every centimetre crawls a warmth that tingles and soothes; the only thing I can compare it to is a hot shower on a cold morning. The moment in which your chill-infested skin loosens under the warmth of the water but extrapolated and infinite. The outside world seems so cold when you are in the warmth. Then I must change back, which is an inevitability that I often fight, going so far as to stay changed when I go to sleep. When I wake up and know I must leave the house I am utterly ashamed, but on mornings where I have nothing to do, that warmth creeps its way over me. It is intoxicating.

I thought that this was just how it would be. Until I met someone. When she sat down on the dusty red cushion next to me, I froze. Soft candlelight and too much wine made the rest of the dive bar fade out of view. The usual rummaging of thoughts cut short. The rest of the crowd whirred around us, and I was not sure who was who anymore. I felt like I was under a thin, sharp spotlight.

I went home with her that night on the tram. It was maybe three in the morning. As we hummed along at the back of an empty carriage, watching the rubbery joint turn the bends before we did, my skin yearned for the change. Her head swayed slightly, mine felt like it was melting on my neck.

Her heels clicked on the pavement as the wind smacked against my dry eyes. Melbourne's winters are cold and quaint; the sun waits a while before showing its face. Inner suburbs, small townhouses and cobbled alleys. We followed a tiny path through the biggest front garden I had ever seen. We moved past the flimsy gate and into the front door. I asked her if she has any housemates. She shook her head and led me up the stairs to her bedroom, a warm carpeted den with posters for things I have never heard of plastered to the walls. Any dead space was filled.

I was shivering as we sat on the edge of her bed, but the room was warm. My jaw chattered. I was terrified of what I thought I had to do. Her weight kneaded the sheets as she fell backwards. I felt myself shrinking to a pinpoint. In all the noise of my brain I failed to hear her ruffling around until a finger slipped under my chin to guide my face around. Lying in the centre of the bed was a shape so vibrant and infinite. With the yank of my arm and the comfort of her touch we changed together.

BRANDON SIMEONI (he/him) is a Naarm-based filmmaker and writer who is drawn to narratives centred around internal and emotional struggle. He has had works showcased in festivals such as Monster Fest and Cineaesthesia with producing credits. Brandon is currently working on his first novel. Find out more @brandonsimeoni (Instagram and Twitter/X).

Chromatic Aberration

Rowan Williams

When you're looking for whales, everything looks like a whale. Actually, everything looks like it *could've been* a whale. The open sea expands across the curved world. K and I are sitting on a plastic picnic blanket near the edge of a cliff, behind the Kiama Blowhole, staring out at the shimmering blue. Tot is curled up by our feet, asleep. We're hoping to see at least one whale pass by the sleepy factories on the coast of Wollongong. I'll be happy to glimpse a splash in the distance.

The people who we're staying with told us that at this time of year thousands of them make their way north, travelling up the coast to warmer waters. We had, similarly, made the trek north towards warmer weather, trying to escape the Melbourne winter for a few days.

So far, it's hard to say if we've seen any. So far, it's been an exercise in peripheral blur. There's movement just outside my field of vision – my pupils dart towards it, focus, and then get distracted by movement just outside my field of vision. Tiny waves recede and collapse into the distance. The horizon is a thin line of sparkling diamonds. It's doing something weird to my eyes, as if it's sawing into them each time they scan across it.

No whales yet (I think).

The horizon is too wide to fit inside my head. I've become used to inner-city Melbourne where there are always buildings or tram lines blotting out the sky. Is it the curve of the earth that I'm seeing, or is it the curve of my eyeballs distorting the space?

The sound of the blowhole thumps through the rock and into our backs. Each thump is accompanied by muffled yelps and applause from the people watching it through their phone screens.

When I close my eyes, the horizon is still there. The yellowish afterimage hovering behind closed eyelids superimposes itself over the actual image when I open them, creating shifting interference patterns, obscuring any whales that I could be seeing.

'Is that one?' K says, pointing towards a wispy pink cloud.

'Near the cloud? That black and white thing? I think it could be a boat.'

'How about over there?'

'Where? Oh yeah... are they waves?'

'My eyes have gone funny,' she says.

'Mine too.'

There's a couple walking along the top of the cliff, pointing out to sea. For a moment I get excited. But then realise that they're probably having the same conversation that we're having.

I've never seen a whale that wasn't on a screen. I've had a thing for whales since I was a little kid. By 'thing' I mean that they're both terrifying and beautiful. I remember glimpsing a scene from *Jaws 3* on TV late one night, possibly when I had the flu, possibly tiptoeing past the lounge room on my way to the toilet (I can't remember) and peering in at the murky cinematography bouncing shadows around the back of the couch. I've since watched bits of the movie on YouTube to check that one, I didn't imagine the scene, and two, it was as murky and disturbing as I remember it. I've confirmed that no, I didn't and yes, it was.

There are no whales in *Jaws 3* (that I can remember) – but what struck me was the gloomy underwater reality presented in the movie. This gloom stuck to my mind and followed me back to my bedroom, where my brother slept on the bottom bunk, and wrapped itself into the fabric of the dim room. I imagined (not actively – these thoughts were automatic) that the room was filled with water, the texture of the movie had spilled into our living space, each shadow was a swarm of film grain and bubbles. The walls dissolved into the endless darkness of the sea. Then, I realised that this was reality *right now* for creatures living underwater. Even writing this now, remembering that imagined shadowy world, the bottom falls out from somewhere within me, triggering something like vertigo. I experience two parallel thoughts: floating alone (as a whale) and having a whale swim next to me (as a human).

'There's one! Oh no, that's a seagull,' K says.

Trails of darker blue crisscross the expanse of the sea, churned up by boats that passed by earlier in the day. The horizon splits the sky in two.

Jaws 3 was originally screened at the cinema in 3D. It was shot using a lens that split each frame in two – the top half recorded what the left eye would see, and the bottom half recorded what the right eye would see. Another lens would then sum the two halves into a doubled whole – two slightly different films playing at the same time. You'd need to wear those crappy '80s red and blue glasses to view the 3D effects. The version that I saw on TV consisted of the top half only – giving the movie the grainy look that seeped into my imagination as a little kid. I can't tell you anything else about the film – not the plot, or the characters, or the meaning. Only that its eerie light still affects the way I see the sea.

The wind picks up. The corner of our little picnic blanket thrashes against the grass. Tot scratches behind her ear. Still no whales.

'It's getting cold,' K says.

'Should we go soon?'

'Maybe. We could come back tomorrow.'

The other couple left a little while ago. A lone seagull hovers against a gradient of lilac and purple in the evening sky. The sea leaks its own light into the dusk. It looks like TV static. The blowhole thumps and no-one claps.

ROWAN WILLIAMS (he/him) is a writer and an editor. He was a member of the working group on the 2020 and 2022 issues of *n-SCRIBE* magazine. Rowan's work was highly commended in the 2020 Darebin Mayor's Writing Awards. He currently lives in Northcote in an apartment that leaks when it rains. Email williams_rowan@outlook.com to get in touch.

Corridor Wars

Mia Ferreira

It was a humid February morning, but Zoe was trembling. She stood behind the door, listening. She pulled it open, stepped through and collided with Pete as he marched out of his room at the same time. He grunted and recoiled sharply, putting as much space between them as the narrow corridor would allow.

Zoe's gaze moved from the basket of dirty laundry in his arms up to his eyes. She could never guess what colour they'd be – a translucent hazel that picked up green or blue, or sometimes grey. They changed as often as the Melbourne weather – and his moods. Today they reflected the green of his loose singlet and would have been lovely to look at, if Pete did not perpetually appear unimpressed and annoyed.

'Sorry,' she blurted, putting up her hands apologetically and protectively, taking a step back to give him more space.

'So you should be,' he grumbled, readjusting the basket on his hip.

'Well good morning to you too!' Zoe had wanted to sound casual with a touch of playful sarcasm, but her voice croaked and then squeaked awkwardly.

Sunday was Pete's only day off, and he had a routine – get up; wash his work clothes, bed sheets and towels; brew a fresh cup of coffee on the stove; and cook a hot breakfast. Then, he would move onto whatever part of the house he felt needed a forensic-level clean that week. One time, he removed all the blinds and curtains, washing and cleaning them in a frenzy, using a whole variety of products and techniques. Another week, he scrubbed and washed every inch of the lounge room walls and ceiling. He was relentless and did not stop for hours. Zoe quickly learned that if she tried to help, he would only accuse her of doing a poor job, but if she didn't offer, he'd complain that no-one else did anything around the house.

The old house was run-down. According to neighbours, it had been passed from one random renter to another for twenty-five years. The carpet was old and stained, and there were scuff marks on the doors and walls that wouldn't come off, but it was spacious, light and airy. It was generally clean and nowhere near as cluttered as most share houses. Zoe had moved in a little over a year ago. Pete had moved in five months ago and quickly asserted himself as the domestic king of the castle.

At first, Zoe thought he was a clean freak or a perfectionist, but every time she peeked into his bedroom, she saw piles of clothes, shoes, plates, cups, books and knick-knacks on every surface. It was like a totally different person lived in that room, but Zoe didn't want to be caught snooping and said nothing.

Everyone knew to stay out of Pete's way on Sundays. The vacuum cleaner and washing line were off limits. Amanda, their other housemate, had started staying with friends or would sneak out on an early bike ride. Ordinarily, Zoe wouldn't have attempted any morning banter, but she expected this day to be different.

Instead, Pete turned abruptly and walked down the corridor without uttering another word.

'Hey, can we talk about last night?' Zoe quickly called out after him, leaning against the wall for support. After her last breakup, she'd promised herself to always speak up and have the difficult and uncomfortable conversations early. This was her first opportunity to put the promise into practice. Always the peacekeeper and master at 'playing it cool', she was terrified but also excited that this next conversation with Pete could represent a turning point for healthier relationships. She couldn't wait to tell her therapist.

'What?' He stopped on the step, halfway between the sunken lounge and kitchen.

'Um, I think we should talk about what happened. I don't want things to be weird between us or anything...' Heat was rising in her face, but she was still shivering.

'Why would things be weird?' he shot back.

'Because we—'

'Oh relax, it's no big deal. We're both adults. These things happen...' And with that, Pete disappeared through the kitchen and out the back door.

Zoe was stunned. She never knew where she stood with Pete. No-one really did. He was unpredictable at the best of times. But his reaction was not what she'd hoped for after the night they'd just shared.

Tension had been steadily building for weeks, as the space between them on the lounge shrunk. Saturday night pizza and wine had become a ritual, along with 'hip-hop karaoke'. They laughed hysterically as they tried to keep up with the lyrics, danced and drank – a lot. It was nice to see Pete relaxed and playful and, while she hadn't admitted it to herself, Zoe had stopped making other Saturday night plans. When he scooped her up in his arms last night, she was unsure if the jolt of electricity was excitement or panic. Before she could react, he'd carried her to bed and lain down next to her...

What happened between them was not planned, but also not totally unexpected. His cold reaction this morning wasn't a big surprise either. When he was up, he was great but when he was down, he was like a destructive toddler who would attempt to bring everyone down with him. No-one knew when or why he would suddenly shift. Like the time he accused Zoe of not taking trivia seriously enough, storming off and leaving her alone at the pub. He didn't speak to her for two weeks, and she thought one of them would have to move out. But it was like he flipped a switch one day, and everything went back to normal.

When Pete first moved in, he'd mentioned a bad breakup and made it clear he didn't want to talk about 'it' or 'her' ever again. Zoe was also being protective with her heart, so as difficult and complicated as he was to deal with, she felt like she understood where he was coming from. Things had been good between them for a while now. They had spent more time together and shared a lot about themselves. Zoe naively thought they would be able to talk about what happened between them and, at the very least, agree to be friends.

Looking around the spotless lounge room, Zoe sensed that something wasn't quite right. The empty wine bottles and glasses, pizza boxes and ice-cream wrappers from the previous night were nowhere to be seen. Something about the perfectly arranged cushions made her feel off-centre and dizzy, and she wondered if it had all been a dream.

MIA FERREIRA (she/her) is a freelance copywriting, public relations and social media consultant who believes in the power of storytelling to connect and inspire. She's also a book reviewer for ArtsHub and a certified Iyengar yoga teacher. When she's not writing, reading or standing on her head, you'll find her outdoors, chasing sunsets and waterfalls. Follow Mia @_miaferreira_ or @oh_my_yoga (Instagram).

Giantsbane

Belinda McDonald

They call me *Nigel Giantsbane*. Or they will once I've figured out how to kill one. They're bloody big, you know.

I come from a long line of Banes. From the first time man and monster crossed paths, my family has left a trail of decapitated beasts in their wake. My father is Frederick 'Fang Crusher' Basiliskbane, and my mother, the infamous Catherine Sirensbane. Even my little sister has taken up the family pastime. A swamp-hag snuck into her room one night when she was sleeping. Had she known that Claudia slept with a small armoury under her pillow, she might have picked a different window. Dad was so proud that he stuffed and mounted the old crone in our hall, the hatchet still embedded in her skull. Every full moon, putrid swamp slime oozes from her eyes like foul green tears. I avoid that corner when I can.

But, throughout our history, nobody has bagged a giant.

I've been studying for months now. I've learned everything the experts have to offer on the subject, including which giants I stand half a chance at slaying. There are plenty of woods around here, so the woodland giants seem like the best place to start. They're the smallest kind, probably so they can sleep in the boughs of the great oak trees without snapping them. They keep to smaller, immediate family units – five at the most – rather than living in large clans of fifty or more. Their claws might be an issue, but they're more for gripping bark than rending flesh. The camouflage is proving to be tricky. My current plan is to lure them out with strategically placed piles of berries. I should probably think of a plan B. If I can't slay a damned woodland giant, I'll have to move on to one of the other clans.

There are plenty of caves around here too, but cave giants are the worst of all. Years of cross-breeding with trolls has given them impenetrable, rocklike skin and a penchant for using human corpses in their interior decoration. I'll be staying far away from caves.

I know everything there is to know about giants. Except, of course, how to kill one.

I asked Dad if he had any ideas, but he just grumbled something between sips of ale about useless sons wasting time on daydreams instead of going out and making names for themselves. It seemed to go over his head that I *was* trying to make the greatest possible name for myself.

Mum was not much better – only half listening as she swung a cleaver through a hellhound's thick sinews and bones. 'Yes, dear. That sounds wonderful. Do be careful, won't you? I don't want my darling pudding getting hurt.'

'Must you call me that?' I sighed.

'Hmm?' She cast an eye over her shoulder, still swinging the cleaver with precision. 'What's wrong with being my pudding?'

'It's not very manly, is it?' I rested my hands on my slightly protruding belly.

Mum's eyes shot down and then back up. 'I think it suits you.'

Dejected, I left the kitchen and made my way to the library. The shelves were packed with stories of brave heroes and their exploits; rescuing princesses and overthrowing evil kings. All that good stuff. I'd spent my early years combing through every volume, absorbing the lessons imparted: be brave; don't give up; truth and justice will always triumph; make sure you've got a bigger sword than your opponent. The stories were all distinct, except for one common thread: not one of these heroes, man or woman, looked like me.

Some were tall, some on the shorter side. There were eye patches, missing legs, scars – you name it. But they were all men rippling with muscle, or slender women who packed a surprising punch for their diminutive size. There were other characters in these tales whose physiques more closely echoed my own, but they weren't the sort a young lad looks up to. Bumbling sorts. Or evil and grotesque. Not the sort one aspires to be at all.

'Which one will it be today, Nige?'

I jumped in surprise – a tad too dramatical to pass off as anything other than what it was. 'Gods, Claudia. Do you have to skulk everywhere?'

She shrugged, twirling one of her thin, blonde braids around her index finger. 'Can't help it.'

'No, I suppose you can't.'

'So, which one?' She ran a finger across the shelves until she hit a familiar edition bound in emerald dragonhide. 'Oh, this one. Please, Nige? I love the voices you do with this one.'

'Not today, little Claw.' I slumped into one of the overstuffed armchairs, shoving the dire wolf pelt draped over it to the floor.

Claudia made a little nest out of the discarded fur, plopped down with her legs crossed, and stared up at me with those big, manipulative eyes. 'What's wrong?'

I let out a long exhale, feeling myself deflate into the seat. 'You wouldn't understand.'

She jabbed my shin with one of her sharpened fingernails. 'Try me.'

'I just… I don't know.' I twisted a loose thread from the armchair into a tight ball and snapped it off. 'Maybe I'm a changeling and nobody noticed.'

I expected her to laugh, but she just sat quietly.

I exhaled. 'I'll never achieve anything.'

She scoffed. 'Rubbish. You're the smartest person I know. Nobody else even comes in here, except to nail new pelts to the wall.'

I shrugged. Having read of all the wondrous feats I could never hope to achieve didn't seem like much of an accomplishment.

'How can I help?' she asked.

Her sincerity brought a reluctant smile to my lips. My little Claw had never met a challenge she couldn't face. Perhaps...

'Want to go giant hunting?'

BELINDA MCDONALD (she/her) is a young-adult fantasy writer and lover of all things speculative fiction. When she's not working on her novel, she's writing book reviews for *Aurealis* magazine, or thinking about dinner.

Simple Dreams *or*
Gay Panic in the Bathroom

Eric Butler

A dive bar that only plays Linda Ronstadt
and I am dancing on a table, wearing the kind
of shoes that click when I walk so people know
I'm coming; pressing against rough denim thighs
new stranger, new scent, no new names tonight.

In 1977 a man's head collided with a sink pipe;
same bathroom, different sign hanging out front.
It didn't make the papers, but there's a dent!

I am unwelcome everywhere except my own
bedroom(!) and grateful to keep paying rent
for the honour.

I am unwelcome in anything other than my
father's clothes, passed down like inter-
generational trauma.

'Blue bayou' plays for the third time that night as
I escape to a cubicle, just to not be seen for one
moment. Time passes differently in isolation, the
symmetry of your face shifts without context –
take two breaths

keep on truckin'

ERIC BUTLER (they/them) is a poet, editor and musician living in
Naarm. Their writing focuses on queerness, disconnect and popular
culture. Eric has worked as editor of *Plaything Magazine*, on the
Voiceworks editorial committee and as an intern at HarperCollins
Australia. They can be found walking down Sydney Road, pouting
into the middle distance. Find them @venus_as_a_boy (Instagram).

Displaced

Stephanie Martin

You were four days away from your fifteenth birthday when you knew something wasn't quite right. Your dad joined you at the kitchen bench, calling your sister over. Uneasiness settled over you; Dad never assembled the family meetings. You tried to meet your mum's eyes for comfort, reassurance, guidance; but she was looking away.

You were sat doing your maths homework, and your whole reality shifted in an instant.

Your mum and you were becoming close. Mother–daughter, yes, disagreeing as most teens and parents do. But now, also friends. A dichotomy that was, at times, difficult to navigate. There were indignant teenage blow-ups, parental orders given. There were also moments of companionship and deep soul understanding.

So when your mum told you with seeming ease that she was questioning her marriage to your dad, the familiar territory became hostile and uncharted. You recoiled from the confession and feigned a toilet visit to conceal the tears welling in your eyes. All you were thinking about was what this meant for life as you knew it. It didn't occur to you that as a fourteen-year-old, you were not meant to hear it.

Not a few months before, you had boasted to your friends that, yes, your parents were still together. In a world of broken families, it never occurred to you that yours could be one of them.

Sure, your parents didn't kiss each other goodbye, or good morning, or just hello like in the movies. But the movies aren't real life, right? And sure, there were fights. But people in relationships fought, right? And sometimes on rare occasions, it skyrocketed to yelling. Fights that reached a fever pitch, which you and your sister could no longer pretend you didn't see.

Are you and Dad getting a divorce? your sister asked, after one particularly bad series of events ending with your parents in a screaming match at the other end of the house, several closed doors between you. *How silly of her,* you thought, *to assume such a thing.*

You don't remember how your fifteenth birthday was celebrated. All you remember is your dad arriving at your home with a moving van and then all his belongings gone.

You remember the tears and the reassurances and the hugs and the *nothing to do with you girls,* and the *we love you.*

Your future family life, once assembled with the certainty of togetherness, now stretched before you like a great, murky and cavernous nothing.

Then things started moving at hyper-speed.

Three weeks after your fifteenth birthday, your mum says your dad had told her *there is someone he is interested in from work.* You're old enough to know that it's too soon.

Your dad's new… friend is nice, and you were raised to be polite. But there's a voice inside of you that's screaming, and you do anything you can to push her down, act normal, this is all normal.

He lied to me, you hear Mum crying, and go to her, barely able to make out her words. You are fifteen years old, standing in front of your violently sobbing mum, hearing her repeat those words, not having the slightest clue what to do. You stand there, in your own state of panic, attempting to hug your mum; you know she loves hugs, but you don't know much else.

She confides in you, her friend–daughter. Your dad's girlfriend's ex had contacted her, throwing barbed accusations around. Whether they were true or not, your mum avoids being in the same room as your dad for the next three years to come.

You grow up quick.

Your mum's confiding continues; sixteen, seventeen, eighteen years old. *He told me he told me he told me.* And you listen; you sympathise, detaching the events from the people. The stories churn in your mind as you lay awake in your bed at night. Do you really need to know? You ask yourself. The answer you come to, years and years later, is no.

You're so consumed by your own emotions, or lack thereof, that your sister is left to her own devices, harbouring loneliness and resentments and sadness. It causes a rift that you don't see until it's almost too late. It takes years to rebuild the trust and the ease you once experienced as best-friend sisters. Only at the point of halfway-mended do you realise why the relationship broke in the first place.

You are twenty-four years old, and you don't trust men. What's the point of letting them into your life, of dropping your wall? For what? They will only hurt you in the end. You mistake your wariness for symptoms of shyness, making any excuse to push away anything with potential, anything real.

I think you're this way because of your experience with your parents. The words pierce your heart. Your best friend is not one to hold back, but nothing else she's said has hit you quite this deep. A pain and an illumination.

I think I like him, but maybe just as a friend. You're twenty-six years old, and your psychologist sees right through you. *Building a wall instils the idea that people are dangerous. It limits experiences and resilience and is toxic.*

But toxic is all you know, isn't it?

Things hadn't been right since four days before your fifteenth birthday, maybe even before. At twenty-six years old, you work at breaking old habits, you let people in. It's hard, tearing down those walls. But you know you need to. They've been there for over ten years of fortification. The pain is your armour, protecting you, making you impenetrable. Only later do you realise it's also working against you, keeping the world at arms-length and shielding you from anything real.

Divorce: the later parts of your childhood packaged into one nice, simple word. It changed you, despite your parents' intentions. Your dad just wanted to be true to himself. Your caring mum navigated it the only way she knew how. You were collateral damage, displaced.

It did change you. But now, how, depends on you.

STEPHANIE MARTIN (she/her) is a passionate bookworm with a deep love for storytelling and the written word, living in Naarm. She can usually be found in front of a page or screen, curled up with her spoiled, fluffy babies (cats), Maple and Lulu, surrounded by her many plants and fish. See what she's reading @books_and_skies (Instagram).

Bad Timing

Michael Nguyen-Huynh

While you're busy reading this sentence: the Earth has travelled five-thousand kilometres around the sun; the washing you've hung up this morning has dried to the touch; your pants have become too tight around the waist; Mrs Withers has given birth to a beautiful baby boy in the early hours of the morning; the fromagerie has run out of cheese; I've finished the book you recommended but I didn't really enjoy it, save for a few passages that I'll email to you later; a cool change has swept across the city, and people are hurrying to put on their coats and jackets; a species of arthropod has gone extinct; scientists have discovered the cure for ageing; viewers have left a matinee screening of *Lost in Translation*, unsure of what to think about the kiss between Scarlett Johansson and Bill Murray; I've stolen your doubloons from under your nose; Mrs Withers's beautiful baby boy has graduated from high school top of his class; another species of arthropod has gone extinct; I've spent your doubloons on the cure for ageing; the rising sea has swallowed the islands of Papua New Guinea; Woolworths has announced another year of record-breaking profits; the rotisserie chicken has fluttered out of your price range; Mrs Withers's beautiful baby boy has married his high-school sweetheart; another Aboriginal man has died in police custody; *Scrabble: The Motion Picture* has won the Academy Award for Best Original Screenplay; I've mastered the sound of one-hand clapping; they've built a new highway that connects Melbourne's western suburbs to the bottom of the ocean; Mrs Withers's beautiful baby boy has lost everything in a rather nasty divorce; I've grown weary of eternal life; civil unrest has threatened to unravel the very fabric of society; cities have gone up in flames; the Earth has started to bleed; the Earth has gone into haemorrhagic shock; the Earth has stabilised for now, but wait, what's that, there's a new private jet that runs on the blood of another species of arthropod; the new private jet has been featured in the latest music video from Abel Tesfaye, otherwise known as The Weeknd; I've worked up the courage to take off my jumper, revealing a T-shirt underneath emblazoned with a particularly witty political slogan; climate change has transformed the planet into a desolate wasteland; Mrs Withers's beautiful baby boy has passed away in his sleep, penniless and alone, in the early hours of the morning; the heat death of the universe has returned all matter across the vast reaches of the cosmos to a cold equilibrium, heralding the absence of life and all meaning.

But you wouldn't have noticed if I hadn't said a word.

MICHAEL NGUYEN-HUYNH (he/him) is a Vietnamese–Australian writer and artist. His works are centred on the disruptive relationships between humans, their habitats and their technologies. He's been printed in *Voiceworks* and featured on *All the Best* – a national radio program showcasing emerging Australian storytellers. Visit him at mickynh.com for more.

About *What You Become*

What You Become is an anthology of fiction, non-fiction and poetry written by forty-six final-year students from RMIT's Associate Degree in Professional Writing and Editing (PWE).

The 2023 edition of the anthology was produced by fourteen students from the Towards Publication editing stream. *What You Become* took twelve white-knuckled, butterflies-in-the-stomach, awe-inspiring weeks to create. Final-year students submitted writing in response to the theme of 'change'. Authors were shepherded through the production process by editors who selected, developed, edited and proofread their manuscripts. Alongside these tasks, editors also managed the schedule of each piece, and took on a team role in production, editorial or marketing.

The *production team* – Alexandra Mushta, Elle McFadzean, Mia Ferreira and Sophia Chan – managed weekly progress meetings and kept the production schedule ticking along. They set the flatplan, liaised with the typesetter, and organised printing and the ebook.

The *marketing team* – Chloe Bloom, Clarisse Stevens, Michael Nguyen-Huynh and Neve Grant – spearheaded the title, wrote the press release and marketing plan, and organised the social media content and book launch.

The *editorial team* – Emma Goodall, Gemma Catarina, Rowan Williams, Sarah Rosina Winkler, Stephanie Martin and Upani Perera – developed resources to frame the editorial process, wrote the anthology's subsidiary content, managed editing queries, worked with the cover designer, and completed the final proofread of the anthology.

The editing stream students received plenty of help from industry experts along the way. Author and editor Samone Amba provided invaluable advice on structural editing, and PWE editing coordinator, Louisa Syme, lent editorial support throughout the semester. Julia Jackson from Readings bookshop in Carlton helped students understand the publishing landscape from a bookseller's perspective. Typesetter Shaun Jury advised on layout protocols, and cover designer Darren Holt revealed how words can transform into powerful images. Most importantly, the students couldn't have gotten to the stage of publishing a physical book without the efforts, wisdom and guidance of the PWE teacher-extraordinaries whose practical know-how of the industry, and expert writing and editing skills, continue to hold the highest of reputations.

It was an absolute privilege to have author and poet Claire G. Coleman write the Introduction. Her words place the anthology in context and expand on its themes. We can't thank Claire enough for being part of the project, and we value her wise words about the industry that we're embarking upon.

Many thanks to teacher and anthology managing editor, Michaela Skelly. *What You Become* wouldn't exist without your boundless enthusiasm and support propelling students towards those looming deadlines. Michaela broke this daunting project down into manageable parts that teams could accomplish together. Thanks for being available to discuss punctuation and Word styles when it was well beyond a reasonable time to be thinking about such things.

Thank you to everyone who submitted their writing to the anthology. What a wonderful experience reading through your

manuscripts and working on them together. It was illuminating putting the skills learned during our time in PWE into a real-life project. The manuscripts transformed from a collective dream into this beautiful physical object that you hold in your hands right now. We're humbled to have had the opportunity to create this book and to join the proud Naarm literary community.

Note: 'Naarm' is the Bunurong and Wurundjeri name for the area where Melbourne is located. Authors have used both Naarm and Melbourne in this anthology.

Milton Keynes UK
Ingram Content Group UK Ltd.
UKHW040732111223
434160UK00004B/281

9 780648 705642